THE WALKERS OF CURWOOD

ALEXANDRA MANFIELD

Spindle
PRESS

First published by Spindle Press, 2022

Title: The Walkers of Curwood/Alexandra Manfield, author.

ISBN: 9780645399431

Cover Design: Shkike/99designs

PROLOGUE

The boy clung to the chains of the old Curwood bridge, water racing in a torrent below him. He didn't see Cassie crouched beneath a spiky bush. She made sure of that. The little gentleman—for that was what he seemed in vest and buttoned short-sleeved shirt—had brown arms and springy-looking legs and a face half hidden by swinging black hair. Cassie watched him pick his way across the mouldering planks, testing the wood where soft edges gave way to the rushing creek. Only the last gap left. The mistake here was to look down. Would he? He pressed his lips together, screwed up his face, and took the leap, sailing onto Cassie's side of the river.

She jumped up and crossed her arms like a pirate. He was trying to board her ship without permission, after all. The boy fumbled his landing and fell with a squelch into the mud, his chestnut eyes wide. Cassie laughed.

She wasn't to know then, of course, that Julian Walcott had been laughed at many times before, by someone much more powerful than a pirate child with twigs in her hair.

1

*C*assie didn't mind that her house was the only one on its street. Pardalote Lane held out just long enough to accommodate her family's small weatherboard home before it tapered off into a walking track that wound through the Curwood and down to the river. She didn't mind, because Julian lived across that river. Julian, who was quiet and kind, and Cassie's closest friend.

The Walcotts were not exactly neighbours. There was the Curwood between them: a small forest of large-girthed oaks, slender birches and maples that had escaped the confines of their arboretum over a century ago and now yielded to a remnant patch of shrubs and wattles. Along the stream that marked the boundary of Julian's parents' grand property were towering gums whose majesty rivalled the colonial plantings of the grounds.

At Cassie's place, the two of them climbed and romped, swung and spun on her rope swing. Her parents gave them iced lemonade to drink and Cassie goaded Julian into bare-foot races across her clover and bee-studded lawn. His lawn was not full of clover. It was neat and short; a wide, graceful arc embracing a long, crushed-stone path to his house. They weren't allowed to run on his lawn. Not that it *was* his lawn, really. Very little of that grand place was for Julian.

Julian's father was a tall man with a peevish, stilted air, who seemed ill at ease outside. In the first year of their growing up together, Cassie saw Mr Walcott only three times. The first was when he shooed her from his garden bed as she stood on tiptoes to wave up to Julian at his window. The second was when she and Julian were making fairy rings under a Japanese maple with white stones from the pathway. He'd stood above them, examining her as one might a horse, and his dismissive *harrumph* before he strode off left Cassie with the distinct impression that he had deemed her wanting.

Julian's mother was a glorious creature. She welcomed the neighbour's wild girl with delight. When she was not painting in her greenhouse, she'd bring them plates of biscuits and cups of chilled milk as they played in the garden, and she would fold them both into her perfumed hugs whenever the urge took her. Her eyes were warm and kind, and unlike any adult Cassie had ever known, she seemed happy to sit with them in the shade of the gnarled old rhododendrons and tell them stories.

She was born in the south of Argentina where it was cold and the boats left for Antarctica. Her parents had moved them up to Buenos Aires when she was only a child, where the climate was kinder and the opportunities greater. The tales she wove of that golden city! With its cobbled streets, its tango, and the curious Obelisco in the centre of it all.

Her name was Violeta Andrea Santiago de Walcott. Julian called her *Mamá*, and she called him *mi hijito, Julián*. There were days when Cassie envied the quick parry of Spanish

4

spoken between them, and yet other days when she would lie in the dappled shade, their singsong words washing over and through her, filling her heart with peace.

"And what about you, Cassie?" Violeta asked her one day. "Are you a Cassandra or a Cassiopeia?"

"I'm just Cassie."

Julian snickered, and Cassie folded her arms.

"Would you like to choose?" Violeta asked, her eyes dancing.

Cassie looked from her to Julian and back again, and could almost see the secret silver cord between them as they shared their delight in throwing the spotlight upon her.

"Choose?"

"Do you want to be a prophetess? Or the doomed, vain daughter of a goddess?"

"I'm not vain!"

They both laughed, throwing back their heads like two horses whose black manes rippled in the sunlight as they snorted and snuffled.

"Ah, *nena*, I do not mean to hurt your feelings."

"You're not vain," said Julian.

Thus mollified, Cassie made her choice.

"I'll be the prophetess."

"Aha, good," said Violeta.

"But what is a prophetess?"

Julian roared again. Julian only laughed when his mother was around.

Julian's father had met Violeta when she was an environmental activist in Patagonia, protesting a proposed new oil well. John Walcott was a surveyor and had been a passenger in a string of cars halted by the protesters. The first time John saw Violeta was through his car window as a police officer attempted to arrest her. The tinted window meant

John could see her, but she could not see him. What he saw thrilled him and prompted him to act in a manner so inconsistent with the character that was now Julian's father that Cassie found it hard to fathom. John Walcott had pushed open his door and dragged Violeta inside the car, insisting to the baffled officer that she was one of his crew.

The first time Violeta met John was when she found herself sprawled on his lap while he ordered his driver to make a U-turn out of the procession and high-tail it to the nearest motorway.

Cassie and Julian loved that story, and Violeta retold it many times for their benefit, and perhaps also for her own. Cassie would always search for something in Violeta's eyes that was sad, now that her knight in shining armour had become what seemed to Cassie to be a stiff, unhappy man, but she could never see it; there was only ever the mischievous twinkle of a storyteller. And so, she came to believe that Violeta really loved Julian's father.

The third time Cassie saw Julian's father was when he came to find her.

It was a still, cloudless morning after a wet and thunderous night. Lyra and Ben, Cassie's parents, had let her sleep in their bed because the noise had been so loud. Her mum had gone to work early, and her dad was in the veggie garden, re-staking the tomatoes and tethering the ragged remnants of the cucumber vines to their trellises. Cassie was out with him, hoping he might forget they'd planned on doing mathematics today. Sometimes, if she looked engaged enough with a project of her own, he'd let the formal side of things slide and it'd be up to Mum to take stock on the weekend, to see where she measured up with the kids who went to school. That was when it was time to involve her mother in a crafting project that was big enough to last them into

Monday. Then she could promise to finish it and have it ready to show her when she returned home from work. Cassie hadn't learnt these tactics early enough to stall her formal reading lessons, and anyway she liked words, but maths was something that neither of her parents seemed to be in a hurry to instil in her.

Violeta liked maths.

"It is the language of the Universe, Cassie!" she'd told her as she whirled her around one day. Cassie had looked up at the shadows and light shifting against the sky and, for a moment, felt the tug of something at the edge of knowing, a secret that could unlock the patterns that danced before her eyes.

Julian liked maths too. Numbers seemed to make sense to him. But like his mother, it was music more than anything that gave mathematics its true purpose. Julian could play the piano like nobody she'd heard, even Violeta, whose tunes were mostly improvised, and who played with a passionate verve. Julian's playing was a particular mixture of precision and soulfulness, as though he had learnt and loved the instrument for many lifetimes before this one.

When John Walcott appeared in Cassie's back garden, she was sure he was an apparition. Men like him did not just appear in one's yard. Cassie's father was surely just as stunned, yet he stood up, wiped the earth from his trousers and reached out his hand.

"Hi, I'm Ben. You looking for some help?"

John Walcott did not shake her father's hand.

"Yes." He cleared his throat. "I was hoping...might your daughter come along with me? Her...friend...my son, Julian. He could do with a...a bit of cheering up."

"Oh, you're our neighbour! I've heard so much about you all from Cassie."

John Walcott didn't smile, and his hands began

smoothing his jacket as though he imagined his clothes were covered in as much dirt as Cassie's dad's.

"Is everything okay, Julian's Dad?"

He turned to look at Cassie in the way an eagle might, having just noticed an unpleasant insect on its newly-preened feathers.

"Oh, you're there. I didn't see you in the grass."

She wanted to roar like a lion then.

"It's his mother. She has had an accident. And Julian wanted to invite you to the memorial service."

Cassie couldn't remember much after that, except Dad holding her and inviting John to please come in and sit down...extending his condolences...*sincerely sorry to hear that. How can we help?* The words were a jumble, and the sky would not right itself.

Violeta.

She met John Walcott's gaze, and Cassie imagined he must be occupying the same upside-down world that she was.

"Julian has locked himself in his room," he said. "I thought maybe he'd come out for you."

Cassie and her dad went to the Walcott's house that day by the road, not the forest. The Curwood would never be the same now that Violeta was not in the world.

JULIAN HADN'T WANTED to see anyone that day, not even Cassie.

At the memorial service, he and his father stood stiffly side by side; two lonely pine trees on a barren hill.

After the memorial, Cassie couldn't visit Julian for weeks. John Walcott had decided it would be best for his son to attend the private school an hour from town, now that his mother was no longer around to educate him at home. So that left only the weekends. Weekends were precious, because for those two sweet days, Cassie's mum was at home. Lyra had to commute so far for work that she often stayed in the city rather than wrangle the traffic or the crowded trains for hours on end.

On this Sunday though, Cassie's mum had an article to write for work and Dad said not to bug her, so she headed through the forest to the Walcotts'.

She found Julian sitting at the end of the bridge on her side of the river. He heard her and looked up.

"Were you on your way to my place?" she asked.

He shrugged. "No."

Cassie found a spot and sat down next to him. He picked up a skinny stick and started breaking it into small pieces.

"Julian..."

"I don't want to talk about her."

She sat beside him, imagining herself surrounded by a host of small forest creatures who'd flee if she spoke. It helped her to be silent enough for Julian.

They didn't speak of Violeta then, or the next time, or the time after that. After a while it became a kind of reflex, as though Cassie had bitten her cheek and now chewed on the other side of her mouth to avoid the sore spot. The habit of not talking about Julian's mother became part of their every day, part of who they were together. Violeta became their beloved and unacknowledged ghost.

JULIAN DID NOT SPEAK Spanish again, and it was a rare thing to see him smile. Over the next few years, Cassie did what she could: brought him around to her place more often, made cubbies with him inside and forts outside, and even let him hold her rabbit's new babies and stroke their silken fur. He was gentle with them and made them grassy nests inside their hutch. They caught water beetles from Cassie's pond and he always made sure they put them back again afterwards so that they could be free. Lyra and Ben fed him nourishing food, and sometimes they all ate dinner in front of the TV; something he wasn't allowed to do at home. None of these things made him smile. Occasionally, Cassie would catch him staring up at the forested hills that lined their valley, and she would see a light in his eyes, as though he saw something up there, something wonderful that she could not perceive, and she knew that if he could have, he would have soared right off, up into their wild green.

It was the last day of November. The rain that had been falling on and off in heavy bursts had moved on, leaving rainbows like bridges across the valley. Cassie chanced the walk to Julian's and found him in the greenhouse, feeding Violeta's orchids. They wandered out into the garden, and he told her his father had signed him up for boarding school for his last three years. He said it with a quiet resignation, only a small ripple on the surface of a deep well.

"But can't you just talk to him?"

He took in a deep breath and looked up at the sky. "Hey, there's a camel, look."

The cloud was already re-shaping itself, its humps curling into wisp-like claws. When Cassie turned back to him, he was wiping his face with his sleeve.

"You don't want to go, Julian. Just tell him."

"He doesn't care. It won't make any difference."

The camel joined up with a dragon and blocked the sun, vanquishing all the rainbows.

"Then *I'll* tell him."

"Don't be ridiculous, Cassie." His tone was short, angry, and the sting of it stunned her.

"Fine!"

She stood up and stalked off, feeling his gaze boring into her back. At the edge of the forest, she broke into a run.

Over the next fortnight, Cassie kept her distance from Julian's place, busying herself with helping Dad plant out the rest of the summer vegetables. The week after that, Mum decided that they should stay in the city for a Shakespeare performance at the Botanic Gardens and for Dad to take her to the new exhibition at the Museum.

By the time they returned, Julian and his father were off visiting relatives over the Christmas holidays. And for the whole of January, Cassie and her parents went camping by the beach. So she didn't see Julian before he left for boarding school. In fact, she didn't see him again for a very long time.

---

2

*C*assie was lying on her stomach on her bed, legs scissoring and whacking the mattress. *Thump, thump, thump.* Her body wanted to move. The air outside was shimmering with the last days of summer, but she'd made a promise to herself; such a secret promise that even her parents didn't know it. She'd promised to her heart of hearts that she would learn mathematics. For Violeta. She squinted and frowned at the numbers and symbols dancing in front of her, trying to make them settle so that she could wrest their secrets from them. *The language of the Universe, Cassie.*

Dad had said a cool thing; that calculus was the maths of change, and since the world is always changing, it'd be smart for us to learn it. He had little else to say about it though, because he'd been quoting someone and didn't know how to do calculus himself.

She closed the hard, shiny cover of the textbook and opened it again, hoping that this time all the squiggles would coalesce into something she could understand. But they didn't. They remained stubborn, unknowable incantations. If only Julian had been here. Her anger with him had faded long ago, leaving only a sore, sad spot where Julian should have been. Perhaps he'd come home for the Easter holidays this year. Maybe.

The sound of deep wingbeats and a creaky *"Kaaark"* made her leap off her bed and run outside.

"Dad! Yellow-taileds!"

Ben looked up from his runner beans and watched, smiling, as the pair of yellow-tailed black cockatoos winged their way across the sky.

"Do you ever get lonely, Dad, when Mum's not around?"

His blue eyes searched her face, and then a crinkly look came to his eyes, the one he got when he was thinking about things he liked.

"I miss her sometimes. But I've got you with me." He put down his basket and came over to squeeze her in a hug.

"I miss her too," she said.

"I know you do. And she wishes she could be here with you."

Cassie drew back so that she could look up into his face. "Why'd you guys never have any more kids?"

He straightened his arms out on her shoulders. "Because one was just right."

"Benjamin!" She folded her arms.

"You want a better answer?"

"Yes."

"Cassie, truth-seeker. I've always loved that about you."

She waited.

"We weren't super-young parents and we wanted to give you a few good years where it was just you. By the time we thought about having another kid, we found we couldn't. Which was all right, really. It meant your mum could stay where she was with work. It was a bit tricky for her getting

13

back into it after all those years she'd spent at home early on."

Cassie frowned.

"Was that answer a bit more complicated than you expected?"

"More boring," she said.

He laughed, and she scooted out from under his arms. The day was far too beautiful for any more maths.

She hadn't been in the forest for weeks. The golden light and insect calls were enticing today. She wandered down the path, revelling in the warm breeze on her bare arms and the tinkle of tiny birds in the canopy.

Maybe because she was walking more slowly than usual, or perhaps because a yellow robin began its insistent call just at the right time from the right spot, but she noticed a small track she'd not seen before, leading off to her right from the main path. Her heart did a little skip with the thrill of her discovery, and she stepped onto the track.

The path headed down towards the water. She followed it, leaping over bracken fronds, ducking under tangled shrubs and around piles of shiny deer scats that appeared here and there along the way. Eventually, she reached the river, and the path turned to run along its ferny bank under tall manna gums. After several minutes, with the forest growing dense around her, she thought of heading back, but the track began to climb, and she figured it'd be easier to follow it up to the road and walk home that way.

But the track didn't lead to the road. Instead, it dipped again and headed deeper and deeper into a thicket of tea trees and paperbark. The forest bird calls sounded more distant now; everything felt muffled and close. She found herself treading quietly, as though a single twig-crack could awaken the ragged and twisted forms of the trees around her and that she would not be welcome when they noticed her.

On the other side of the thicket was a circular clearing of yellow grass ringed by white-barked gums. The forest was dark all around it and sunbeams angled into the grassy space. There was movement in the clearing. She ducked behind a patch of tall bracken, her heart loud in her ears.

Two shining creatures stood within the circle. At first, she took them for small, black horses, but quickly realised they were, in fact, tall hounds; slick and wolf-like. She knew so little about dogs that she couldn't even guess at the breed. One began nudging and circling the other, who was sitting on its haunches, and she watched, fascinated, as the other got to its feet and together they began a kind of slow-motion play; tails wagging, bodies rising, falling, circling, mesmerising Cassie with their strange and graceful dance.

It felt like hours, though it may only have been minutes, before the larger of the two raised its nose to the air as though it had caught the scent of something. It took a moment for her to realise that the scent was likely her own. Shivers ran cold up and down her arms. She edged back towards the tea trees, cursing the cracking bracken beneath her feet, and as soon as she reached the thicket, turned and ran. A long, low howl started up behind her. She screamed and tore along the track, tripping and stumbling over roots and deer poo, past whipping, scratching branches, fearful that at any moment she would hear the pounding of paws against the ground behind her or feel claws ripping into her back.

Finally, she reached the main path and swung towards home, running faster than she ever had before. She thrust open the gate, raced through the back garden where there was no sign at all of Dad, ran into the house, slammed the door, and raced upstairs to the safety of her bedroom.

~

CASSIE DIDN'T TELL Dad about the dogs. She wasn't sure why she didn't. Perhaps it was because the whole event felt like a dream, a bubble of a world within this world, something she couldn't hold on to or examine because it was a shimmering thing, slipping up and away from her. And she might have thought it a dream if it weren't for her heart that was still thumping or the sweat that was cooling and tingling now on her upper lip.

"Cassie!"

It was Dad's voice from the study.

She took in a deep breath and blew it out, ran her fingers through her hair; four or five dried leaves were tangled into her curls. Cinnamon curls, her mum called them, for the mid-brown colour of Cassia bark that was the exact shade of Cassie's hair. Cassie had always presumed Lyra was describing their colour and not their scent. It had never occurred to her to ask. She could smell the forest's resinous fragrance in her room. More eucalyptus than cinnamon; a spicy, wild scent. She pulled out the tiny leaves and laid them one by one along the windowsill.

"Cassie, can you come here a minute?"

"Coming!"

Dad's study was one of Cassie's favourite places. She loved the way the sun hit the mud-brick walls in the afternoon. At this angle, the light lit up the little white shells that he and Mum had placed inside the bricks and which, for years, Cassie had thought were fossils.

He had papers lying across one side of his desk next to his

PC. On the other side were wooden figurines at various stages of creation, and on the low shelf behind his desk was one of Cassie he'd finished years ago. She loved its smoothness, the rounded cheeks of the girl she was, and the way he'd worked the grains of the wood so that they looked like fine strands of wispy toddler hair.

"I've just been on the phone to Mum."

Cassie frowned. There was something strained about him, a tightness in his voice.

"Is she okay?"

"Oh, yes, she's okay. She's just...they need her to stay onsite longer. For another fortnight. It's a big project. They're all running to a deadline and there are going to be some long hours in the office...Cassie, don't...Cassie."

Cassie was hammering her fist into the wall. She couldn't help it. It felt good to pummel something, and it helped to drain away the shaky energy left in her body from the forest.

"I know you miss her. She doesn't want to stay. It'll just mean she doesn't have to go in after that for a good while once the project's done. Cassie, please stop."

It was the quiet sadness in Dad's voice that brought Cassie up short. She stopped her hammering and leaned against the wall.

"Dad..."

"I know, darling. We're both going to miss her." He sighed. "There's one other thing though."

Cassie glared at him, and he seemed to flinch as he turned back to the computer screen.

"Mum agrees with me that we need a tutor."

"What?"

"We're both worried that you're not where you should be in your studies. At school they're doing their VCE at your age."

The world began to spin. "But you can teach me!"

"You know I'm not good at that sort of stuff really."

"Yes, you are! You teach me heaps!"

"Look, it's either this, or...school."

Cassie widened her eyes as she stared at her dad sitting so meekly in his office chair.

"Dad, what have you been looking up?"

"That's what I wanted to show you."

He shifted the screen towards her. The face of a young woman stared out from an oval-cropped photograph. She looked—and Cassie hated she was even thinking this—cool. Her hair was short and black, pixie-ish. She wore a green jacket over an olde-worlde lacy top. Her eyes were the weirdest colour Cassie had ever seen: a shining grey that was almost silver.

"Who is she?"

Dad must have noticed the begrudging admiration in her voice, because she felt the tightness in him ease a little and his voice soften out.

"Maybe your new tutor? What do you reckon? Her name's Alisa. But she says here that you can call her Ali for short."

THAT NIGHT, Cassie threw open her window. The sky was a dark velvet. On the horizon, behind the great hulk of the forested hill across the valley, she could just see the yellow glow of the rising moon. Within minutes, its molten edge was silhouetting the outer canopies of the tall mountain trees, rising above them with spectacular speed, as though impatient to get to its night's duties. This was the moment Cassie had been waiting for. It was one of the few times she could feel the earth turning. The moon wasn't rising; she was falling forwards, head over her heels. She felt herself somersaulting through the sky until the moon was lost above the jutting beams of the roof.

She threw herself onto her bed.

A tutor.

Maybe it'd be good? Maybe.

There was a hollow feeling in her chest. Her mother's face flashed across the black screen of her mind. For that moment she saw her clearly: her long, auburn hair, straight though, not wavy like her own; her hazel eyes, sometimes blue, sometimes green; and the way her cheeks indented and curved around her mouth when she smiled. Lyra was a eucalypt. And she was the Cassie who lived in her branches. There'd been a time, long ago, when her mother had taken her everywhere; carried her against her body wherever she went. The shops, the garden, the forest. To this day, the rhythm of her walking heartbeat, of sunlight flashing through trees, was what Cassie returned to when she needed to feel safe.

Two weeks. Too long. She knew enough about normal teenagers to know that most people her age longed to be away from their parents, but she had never felt that with Lyra. With her mother nearby, things felt easy and magical, and everything made sense. Without her, the world was a little less bright, a little less golden.

She would once have visited Julian, confided in him. He would have had her spilling out her fears and worries so that they could both see them. He'd always had a way of fashioning heavy things into smaller pieces that were easier to carry. But, of course, Julian wasn't there. Just sad, old Mr Walcott, who'd sent his son to the lions. Old anger like lava welled up from her stomach. She should tell him he'd done a bad thing, sending his son away. Tell him that Julian was going to die being trapped like that. But of course, she could never tell John Walcott those things. Any more than she could convince Dad she didn't need a tutor, or Mum that she should come home.

3

The day the tutor arrived was not one of Cassie's finest, even by her own standards. Dad hadn't been able to entice her from her bedroom all morning. He had tried the help-me-in-the-garden card with a new row of late basil that needed planting out, and then, when that hadn't worked, he'd banged around in the kitchen downstairs whipping up his specialties: melted cheese muffins, and banana smoothie. But Cassie was unmoved. The grey drizzle outside matched her mood. She lay on her bed, making animal patterns out of the wood grain in the roofing boards above her head. The eyes of crocodile, fox and whale all seemed appropriately mournful.

Eventually, Ben started streaming music from the study. Blaring jigs and reels and folky fiddle tunes battered at her ears.

She tore open her bedroom door. "Turn that down!"

Her dad's grinning face appeared from around his door frame.

"You look stupid!"

She regretted her words as soon as they'd left her mouth, but she still wanted to yell at him, so she banged her door shut again.

He turned the music down, but not before Cassie had picked up her maths textbook and thrown it across the room. It landed like an injured bird; its white dove wing pages all sad and askew against the skirting board as the music stopped.

Then the doorbell rang.

Though she would never quite know whether her new tutor had waited until the rumpus had died down before ringing the bell or whether her timing was simply a fortuitous accident, the memory of their first encounter would always douse Cassie with a hot wash of shame.

Cassie watched from the top of the stairs as Dad opened the door. She could just see the top of the tutor's head. Her hair looked as it had in the photo, dark and cropped short. Her skin was pale and smooth, like one of those TV ad models who bathed in dandelion milk soap or some other ridiculous ingredient. Dad finished his greeting and stepped aside to usher her in.

Before she was fully prepared for it, the tutor's strange, silver gaze located Cassie leaning against the banister.

"Hello, Cassie. I'm Ali."

Her voice was a surprise. It was the voice of someone who knew what it was to be alone and to like it, the voice of someone approaching a deer in a forest; quiet, and shaped like a river, with no sharp edges.

Dad jumped into the silence that followed with his happy mode on. "Well, shall we go hang in the kitchen? Cassie and I were about to have a bite to eat. Why don't you join us?"

"Sure. I'd love to." Ali winked at Cassie.

Before this, Cassie would have said, had anyone asked, that the time between introduction and first wink should be at least a month. Yet somehow, this wink felt okay—good, even—as though she was being let into a secret club. She followed them into the kitchen, found the furthest stool from her dad and began wolfing down her cold cheese muffin.

THE TUTOR WAS to start the next day. Not too early, as Dad was keen to keep Cassie's mornings calm and unhurried. Even Cassie had agreed with him on that point. Sleep was good, and her household liked a lot of it. Dad sometimes went to bed not long after sundown if he could manage it. Things got a bit later when Mum was home though, because then they would all sit together at the table to eat and chat.

These were some of Cassie's favourite times. One of them usually brought up some puzzle from the day to be nutted out, whether it was why the snow peas in the backyard were doing so much better than those in the front, how the Roman Empire met its demise, or what was on the other side of a black hole. The dictionary had been brought out so many times at dinner that it now sat permanently on the shelf with the cups and mugs, and the rule of no devices at the table had been bent so out of shape to accommodate 'quick' internet searches, that Lyra had eventually donated their huge set of the Encyclopaedia Britannica to the local library.

Cassie was nervous as the clock ticked around to ten am. Once again, she wished she could have talked to Julian. Just a quick chat on the phone would have helped. She didn't even know if he had his own phone now, or whether he'd even be allowed one at boarding school. She certainly hadn't managed to convince her own parents yet that she needed one.

She pulled on the cleaner-looking of her two pairs of jeans, threw on a t-shirt and raced downstairs into the garden. It was a warm, blue-sky day. Dad's sunflowers seemed to have grown overnight. She stood against them to see who was taller.

"You, by a centimetre."

Cassie peered around the sunflowers. The tutor was swinging open the gate, smiling. She felt her cheeks flush with annoyance. How had she arrived so quietly?

"Are we starting with maths, then?"

"Do you want to?"

"No."

The tutor raised her eyebrows.

"I want to start with chocolate chip cookies. Come on. Dad made some this morning for us."

The tutor laughed. It was a real laugh. That was a relief; Cassie hated it when people did those fake laughs. You could always tell.

After morning tea, which somehow had Dad pulling out his banjo while Cassie groaned with embarrassment, she led Ali back out into the garden. Dad had set up a small table with pens and notebooks and two chairs for them to work outside in the shade.

"All right. What would you like to work on, Cassie? Shall we go with what excites you the most? Or with what you're finding hardest to get your head around right now? I'm happy to be guided by you."

This wasn't quite what Cassie had expected. But she thought about it seriously. Writing, drawing, and making stuff with her hands had felt fun and fairly effortless for her.

She'd always envied Julian's musical abilities. But she wasn't sure whether Ali knew anything about music. Dad did. He'd tried teaching her a few things on the piano. She kind of knew that she'd probably enjoy it and be okay at it if she tried. No, it wouldn't be useful for her to ask Ali about music. That left maths. Violeta's face flashed into her mind, and she thought of the wounded textbook lying on her floor.

Ali cocked her head to one side and searched Cassie's face. Could she sense Violeta's ghost? Cassie frowned and looked down.

"I would like to learn maths. I should be up to Year 11. But I'm not, yet."

"That sounds like a fine plan," said Ali. "We shall start with maths."

They spent all afternoon in the garden that day and for the rest of the week. They began with the basics so that Ali could work out what level she was working at, using cherry tomatoes and calendula flowers when they needed to make things tangible. Ali was kind and patient and had a way of sensing when Cassie was frustrated. At these times, she would stop them for a break, get Cassie running or climbing. She told her jokes and made sure she ate and drank.

They moved onto graphs shaped like hills and valleys and umbrellas, and finally, Cassie was shading under curves and learning the words of calculus. Integration, differentiation—they sounded like incantations to Cassie, as though she and Ali were calling up some universal magic, the beginnings of a secret path that if Cassie followed it far enough, could lead her to a place where space and time ceased, a place where Violeta still existed.

"Are you doing something fun on the weekend?" Ali asked her on Friday as they sat sipping peach iced tea.

"No, not really. Mum's still going to be away."

"Do you have any friends nearby?"

"No. Not anymore."

"Oh, really?"

"Yeah. He's gone to boarding school. We used to hang out all the time."

"I'm sorry to hear that. What's his name?"

"Julian." To say his name hurt a bit. Cassie frowned and took a sip of her tea.

Ali sat back. "You're good friends by the sounds of it."

"I dunno now. We had a fight before he left. And I never got to say sorry."

"Oh, Cassie, that's rough."

"Yeah." A jolt of excitement ran through her then. "Hey, do you want me to show you the forest? I could show you his house. It's really beautiful. It's a big old place with pretty gardens."

Ali sat forward again, her eyes luminous. "Sure, why not?" They slurped down the rest of their iced tea and jumped up.

"I'll just go tell Dad."

By the time Cassie had returned, Ali was outside the front gate with a wide, conspiratorial smile on her face. Cassie felt a glow of warmth for her tutor and the restless feeling in her body that told her it was time for an adventure.

But as they reached the edge of the forest, her heart started thumping. Somehow, she'd pushed aside the memory of the giant dogs, but now the thought of their howls behind her made her shiver. Ali noticed.

"You okay?"

She took a deep breath. "Yep. Let's go in. It's this way."

When they got to the bridge with no sign of anything bigger than a thrush along their way, Cassie felt her tension ease.

"Do you wanna come across with me?"

"Of course," said Ali.

"Just be careful, it's a little slippery in places."

The water seemed a little faster and higher than usual with all the unseasonal summer rain and the bridge wobbled more with a grown-up on it. Cassie had the momentary vision of it snapping beneath them. But luckily, Ali was a skinny kind of grown-up, and they reached the other side safely.

Cassie ran to the opening in the forest that was the border of the Walcott's property.

"Wow!" Ali was behind her. "I see what you mean! Who'd have thought this grand old place was nestled in here?"

"Neat, huh?"

"Who lives here now?"

"Just Julian's dad; grumpy old John Walcott."

They crept forward, stepping softly across the mossy areas between the big old rhododendrons that Cassie, Julian and Violeta had spent so many days picnicking amongst. It felt so different without them. Colder. As though the trees and shrubs were turned inwards, keeping themselves to themselves, grumbling to each other about strangers.

"Let's go back," whispered Cassie, more sharply than she had intended.

"Yes, let's." Alisa turned around. "Feels a bit funny doesn't it."

Perhaps it shouldn't have surprised her by now to know that Ali could feel these kinds of things too. It was just that so many people couldn't.

They hurried across the bridge and Cassie felt much better once they'd made it back to the proper side.

The sun flooded the forest floor with a diffuse golden light as they wandered back home.

"Ah, I love a forest when it's like this," Ali said, skipping ahead along the track.

"I know! Isn't it beautiful! Doesn't it almost make you believe in elves and fairies?"

Her tutor turned and smiled, her silver eyes uncanny in the forest's glow. "It sure does."

4

That weekend, Cassie found herself, somewhat to her surprise, missing Ali almost as much as her mother. She had become used to her tutor's encouraging presence. Also, she'd managed a chat with Mum on the phone the night before, and just hearing her voice had been enough to bring Cassie her first good, deep sleep in a while.

Dad was tackling a new carving project, a big one in the garden. It had started the day as a rough block of wood. Since the early morning she'd been hearing the scraping of his tools as he whittled and shaved.

She wandered out in her pyjamas with her mug of orange juice.

"What's it going to be?"

He jumped. "Oh, didn't hear you! Sorry Cas. What'd you say?"

"What are you making?"

He straightened, shaking some curls of wood off his shirt.

"You know, I'm not actually sure yet."

"Looks like an animal."

"Yeah, I think you're right, Twigs."

He hadn't called her Twigs in years. She frowned. He was flushed and sweating with the effort of his task.

"Do you need some water?"

"Yeah. You know, I do. I'll come in with you. Come on, let's get some brekkie."

She sat at the breakfast bar watching Dad pour soy milk into pancake flour.

"Is everything okay?"

He flicked a surprised glance at her.

"Yes. Yep. All good."

She nodded. "Okay."

They ate their pancakes in silence at first. Then Dad switched on his music. Cassie got up and switched it back off.

"Cas? What—"

"Spill the beans. What's wrong?"

He sighed.

"Your mum's going to be away longer. They want her to go interstate for a bit. I'm sorry. She was going to tell you herself last night when she called, but I didn't want her to just yet, not after your last..."

Cassie felt her lips tighten, her heart constrict. She gripped her glass. "Dad, it's okay."

"It is?"

Cassie nodded, just once; it was all she could muster. "When does she leave?"

"Day after tomorrow. We'll call her again before she goes, wish her luck..." He let out a long breath. "It's just...well, I know you must be so lonely. With no friends your own age, nothing to do here. I've been thinking—"

"I'm not going to school." Cassie surprised even herself

with the firmness of her voice. "You gave me a choice and I am still making that same choice."

He sat back, crossing his arms. "The thing is...maybe we shouldn't have given you that choice so early in your life. Maybe it wasn't really yours to make then. And these are important years at school, you know, the years that help you get into university. If you want to."

Cassie could feel heat rising to her cheeks. "No. You guys did the right thing."

He uncrossed his arms.

"Besides, I like Ali. I think she's good. She's helping me a lot."

He nodded. "All right. We'll give it another month. Reassess when your mother comes home. Okay?"

Cassie sensed there was no use in pushing too hard right now. Hopefully, she just had to hold out until Mum got back. Whenever that was going to be.

"Okay."

ON SUNDAY NIGHT, she had to wait a long time for the moon to rise. It was after eleven o'clock before the first sliver appeared above the hill. Her window was open wide, and she could hear all the night sounds of the valley. The cicadas had finished their calling now and there was only the whir of crickets in the grass and the occasional shaking branch as possums made their way through the leafy canopy.

As the moon rose and Cassie was trying to guess the number of days until it was full, she caught a hint of movement in the garden below. She looked down. Dad's sculpture-in-progress glowed pale in the growing moonlight. Was it only the sculpture she had seen? She tried to see into the grainy darkness. Nothing there. She looked further out. Was that something? There! A piece of the night; something denser than shadow was moving just outside their low wire fence, beneath the tall shrubs that lined the boundary of their property.

A huge, black dog stepped into a pool of moonlight.

She gripped the window ledge as she watched the creature snuffle around the gate. Its coat glistened, snaking the light into white ripples in the dark as it paced up and back along her fence-line. Then it lifted its head towards the forest, froze for a moment as though listening to something, and bounded away up the path.

Shivering, she prised her fingers from the sill and reached out to pull the window closed. A second movement caught her eye: someone running along the path after the dog. It was too dark to see properly, but it looked like a slight figure. A child? Or a woman, perhaps? Within seconds, they had both vanished, one after the other, into the enfolding darkness of the forest.

CASSIE SLEPT until late on Monday morning and was awoken by Dad, who rarely disturbed her sleep, knocking on her bedroom door.

"Come on Cas. Alisa will be here soon."

She groaned and rolled over. Webs of her dream were still floating around. It had been a red dream. Lots of red. Intense.

"Cassie!"

She sat up with her eyes still closed and groped around for her clothes.

Eventually she made her way downstairs, her head full of cotton wool and her limbs, heavy.

"What's up with you, Bed-Hair? Late night on the turps?"

"Ha ha, just pass me my coffee."

Dad poured her some orange juice.

"Here. Seriously though. Alisa will be here any minute."

Cassie rested her head against the counter. The wood felt good and cool against her cheek. "I don't want to do anything today. Can you get her to come tomorrow instead?"

"Nope."

She was about to protest when the doorbell rang.

Dad answered it and Cassie heard Ali's bright morning greeting.

"Ugh." She pressed her forehead into the countertop and closed her eyes.

CASSIE EVENTUALLY GOT out of her pyjamas and joined Dad and Ali in the garden. When Dad withdrew to his office, Ali didn't press her with questions; she just wrote out some exercises and allowed the peaceful twittering of the birds and the scented garden breeze to work their magic.

Half an hour later, the quiet of Ali's company was broken by the roar of a vehicle pulling up at the end of the lane. The engine cut, a door slammed, and Cassie's gate squeaked open.

"Where's your father, girls?"

Ali looked mildly at the man towering above them.

"Who's asking?" Cassie squinted up at him.

The man was tall and wide and dressed in a dark cotton drill shirt and black jeans. His broad face was whiskered all around with a metal-grey beard that matched his hair. But the most distinctive thing about him was the huge, white cockatoo that was perched on his shoulder as though he were a pirate.

The man noticed Cassie staring.

"Injured her wing. Can't fly, so I bring her with me."

"Wow! What's her name?"

"I just call her Bird."

"Original," said Ali.

The man narrowed his eyes at her. "Doesn't pay to get too sentimental."

Ali shrugged.

"Now, I'm after Ben. D'you know where he is? He's got a pipe for me to fix."

"Sure, I'll go get him." She exchanged a glance with Ali, who gave her a small nod.

When she returned with Dad, the cockatoo was nibbling on the man's ear with its stumpy tongue and Ali was nowhere to be seen.

"She said to get on with your homework and she'll be back in a bit," said the man.

"Thorne, is it?" said Dad, extending his hand. "Thanks for coming." They shook hands and walked inside, leaving Cassie to her numbers.

By the time Ali returned, it was well after Thorne the plumber had left. Cassie had given up solving for x and was lying in the grass reading a book. She scrambled to stand, but Ali waved her back down.

"No need, you look super comfy down there." She sat cross-legged next to her. "Let's have a snack."

Ali gave her a white paper bag. It was warm, with patches transparent with oil. She opened it and pulled out a cinnamon donut.

"Oh heaven! Thanks!"

34

Ali winked and reached into her own bag.

Cassie ate dreamily, licking the sugar off each finger, trying to savour every crunchy crystal and spongy crumb.

"Any word from Julian?"

The question sent a little jolt through Cassie's stomach. "No. He might come back for the holidays, but I'm not sure. He didn't last year."

"What's that, a fortnight away?"

The colours in the garden seemed a little brighter all of a sudden. "That's kind of soon, actually, isn't it? I didn't realise. No need for school terms here."

"Did you ever go to school?"

Cassie shook her head. "For a bit, when I was little."

Ali nodded and tilted her head to one side, as if waiting for her to continue.

"I hated it."

"Why?"

"I guess, because, well, I always wanted to move around. Do stuff. Not just sit there. You know?"

Ali smiled. "I understand that feeling. I always felt that way too. But I allowed myself to be tamed."

Cassie laughed, though Ali seemed quite serious.

"Yeah, that's it. Tamed. Anyway, Mum and Dad said I didn't have to keep going. So, I didn't."

"And now here you are, in your garden, eating donuts in your maths lesson."

Cassie grinned. They ate a second donut each in silence.

"How was that bird guy? Weird, huh?" said Cassie.

Ali's mood seemed to shift. "Certainly a curious character." She stood up and stretched. "All right, let's get a bit more done before we finish up, shall we?"

5

The next week floated by in a daze of heat that left the garden thirsty and Cassie lethargic. Ali's visits had settled out into a twice-a-week rhythm, and Cassie found herself looking forward to them more than anything. She hadn't become any more enamoured with maths, but the young woman's company brightened her days.

Today was an Ali-free day though, and Cassie was picking calendula flowers to dry for tea when Thorne the plumber returned, this time without his cockatoo, but with a letter for her dad.

"Got yer dad's invoice," he called out over the noise of his car motor.

Cassie jogged up to the gate.

"Thanks, I'll give it to him." She took the envelope. "Where's Bird?"

"Had to leave her at home. Got an injury."

"Oh no, what happened?"

"I dunno. Wasn't there to see it. But I reckon it was a dog attack."

Cassie's eyes widened. A memory of the black dog at her front gate flashed into her mind.

"That's terrible! Is she going to be okay?"

"Yeah, she's a tough one. Once she's grown back her tail feathers she'll be right as rain."

Cassie frowned. "Do you live close by? Only, the other night I noticed a dog I hadn't seen before. It was huge, black I think, though I couldn't tell because it was night."

"Yep, I live just up aways from you, off the High Street. I reckon there's more than one of them. They'd be strays living off rabbits by the river." He pointed his thumb over his shoulder at the forest behind him. He must have noticed her shudder. "Don't worry about them dogs though. They'll keep to themselves. My Bird was probably slinging insults at them. She's got a right tongue on her."

Cassie let out a nervous laugh.

"All right, well, I'd best be off. You make sure your old man gets that, okay?" He folded his broad frame back into his vehicle and drove off.

THAT AFTERNOON, it was too hot to stay in the garden. Even Dad retreated inside.

"I'm going down to the swimming hole," she said when she saw him come in.

The swimming hole was really just a deep, calm spot in the river, downstream of the bridge.

"I can't right now, Cas. Can we go later, when I've finished up for the day?"

"I can go on my own."

A small frown flickered across his face.

"I don't think so."

"But you used to let me go with Julian all the time!"

"Yes, but Julian's not here right now."

He must have realised the many ways that stung, because his face softened, and he met her gaze. "I'm sorry."

"I won't do anything stupid."

He sighed. "Go. Enjoy yourself. But if you're not back in an hour, I'm coming to find you. All right?"

"I'll be back. And I'll be sensible. Promise."

The forest was a lot cooler than the garden. Still, the birds were quiet and even the insects sounded drowsy as she wandered along the path to the river. As she rounded the last bend in the trail, she heard a splash from up ahead. Was there someone else at her waterhole? She paused and peered around from behind a tree next to the path. If there were strange kids there or fishermen, she wasn't sure she'd be so keen after all.

There was something on the bank down by the water. It looked like a sleeping dog, but no, she had dogs on the mind. It wasn't a dog. She craned forward for a better look but something tugged at her from behind. She whipped around to find her towel caught on a shrub. With relief, she untangled it and peeked around for a second look. It was a person. Lying out in the sun, skin a gleaming white. Strange. What she had seen a moment before had looked black and glistening. Perhaps there were two people. Or they'd been in shadow. She was tempted to turn around and go home, but the thought of the cool water was enticing enough that she decided to brave the intruder.

As she approached the bank, she tried to make her footfalls loud enough to wake the person if they were asleep. She was glad she did, because the figure, a woman with short, dark hair, immediately sat up and pulled a towel around herself.

"Cassie!"

It was Ali.

"Phew! I thought there might be fishermen at my swimming spot."

"This is where you swim?"

Cassie nodded and laid out a towel on the bank. "It is. Sorry if I surprised you."

Ali laughed. "I knew I was taking a chance having a skinny dip. I'm just glad it was you!"

Cassie grinned. "You're brave. I'm going in!"

She flicked off her sandals, immersed her feet briefly in the water at the edge, and then dived in. The cold was a shock, as always, but she'd been down here enough times to know it was best to get the pain out of the way as quickly as possible. In a minute or two, she'd adjusted to the river's icy temperature and was happily swimming across to the other side. She loved the freshness of it, the peppermint smell in the air. Floating on her back with the sun streaming orange through her closed eyelids, every part of her felt alive.

She paddled back to the bank where Ali sat, fully clothed now in a green dress patterned with yellow flowers.

"Better?"

Cassie emerged, dripping. "The best!"

"Here, want some?" Ali offered her some purple grapes from a cold bag.

She thanked her and took a handful. "I haven't seen you down here before."

"I haven't been here before. I've only recently moved to the area. I'm still exploring it."

"So, we're neighbours?" Cassie felt something bright light up inside her at the idea.

"Almost. I've rented out a cabin at the caravan park for a while."

"I know the one! You can walk to it from here."

"You sure can."

"Can I come and visit you one day?"

"Of course. If your dad says you can."

"Oh, he will."

Ali looked at her sideways. "Would your mother?"

Cassie scowled. "Probably. But she's not here right now, so who's to say?"

"You miss her." It wasn't a question, exactly. "She must trust you though, to let you go for walks in the forest on your own.

"Well, you know what mums are like."

"What are they like?"

Cassie glanced up at Ali. What sort of question was that?

"Just, you know, mum-ish."

Ali laughed. It was a gentle laugh, but Cassie wasn't quite sure that she wasn't laughing *at* her.

"Well, you're welcome to come around anyway, Cassie." She stood up. "I'd best get going."

Cassie jumped up too. "Oh jeepers! I have to go too. See you next week!"

The forest felt cool and green and magical around her as she sprinted home.

THE DAY WAS cold with the first taste of autumn and Cassie was out gathering tomatoes when Julian returned. She'd straightened to twist her hair up and out of her eyes when she saw him, hands in pockets, leaning against her gatepost.

"Julian!"

She ran and launched at him with a ferocious hug, but he remained rigid, his posture an unfamiliar mixture of awkwardness and aloofness. She let go, heat rising to her cheeks. Had it been too long? Had she done something wrong? Were hugs not a thing they did now?

"Hi, Cassie."

His voice sounded deeper, and he was a full head taller than last time she'd seen him.

"You're way taller than me now!"

"Yeah, I guess." He shrugged and looked down, scuffing at the dirt with his shoe.

"Um...so how's the school?"

He shrugged again. "S'okay."

Cassie felt a hot flicker in her chest. "Just okay? What are the other kids like? Is it weird sleeping there? Are the teachers nice? Why didn't you come and see me last year at all?"

He shook his head like a bridled horse, and she was pleased to see at least some emotion in his eyes now, even though she was pretty sure that what she'd just seen was a flash of irritation.

Yet his tone remained even, almost bored. "So many questions Cassie."

"Julian! Welcome back!" her dad hollered from the porch.

Julian waved as Ben came out into the garden.

"Hi, Mr O'Connell."

"Ben, please! You've known me long enough. Do you want to come inside for a drink?"

Julian shook his head. "No. Thanks. I've got to head back."

"How long are you home for?" Ben asked.

"We have a two-week break. Then I go back."

"It's been quiet around here without you. Are you doing all right?"

Julian nodded. Ben clapped him on the shoulder.

"Good lad. If you need anything, anyone to chat to, you know we're here, right?"

Julian's gaze flickered quickly to Ben's and then back down to his feet. He nodded again.

"All right then, I'll let you and Cassie catch up."

Julian watched her dad go back inside.

"Are you really okay?" Cassie asked quietly.

He flinched almost imperceptibly. "Yeah. I'm fine. I'd better get back."

She frowned. "Julian, I've really missed you."

His dark eyes met hers with an inscrutable gaze. "I've missed you too."

Then he was off, striding back along the track that led to the forest. She watched him go, with a heavy, knotted feeling in her chest.

6

---

*S*eeing Cassie again had been a mistake. She'd been all he'd thought about, the dream he'd lived in as he waded through the punishing days at the new school.

His arrival had aroused some interest in the boys already boarding there. Some of them had heard of the Walcotts, had seemed keen to forge alliances with him on the basis of the wealth and status of his name alone. Yet that was as far as it extended, because for these young men, already aware that they were the elite of the elite, already adept at cutting deals and speaking in the language of snakes and lawyers, there was no such thing as friendship. Not that he would have wanted it. He already had a friend, and she wasn't here.

Yet, now he was back, the sight of her was like a knife to the chest. She had changed. All in good ways, yes, but he hadn't been prepared for it. Her face had lost its childhood roundness. Her hazel eyes, flecked with green, gold and blue, the strength of her presence; these had not changed, but now she was a juxtaposition of hard and soft; her mouth, a woman's. Mrs Darling's 'sweet, mocking mouth' with its hidden kiss. But he was no Peter Pan. He *wanted* to grow up. To become strong and worthy of Wendy.

There was the other thing too, the blossoming certainty that she was no longer safe here. He couldn't quite be sure, but the part of him that could track a scent for miles, that would never let up on a pursuit once begun—*that* part knew. It also compelled him; wanted more and more as he stood and watched her uncertain eyes, saw the dilation of her pupils and heard the uptick of her pulse. And it was threatening to emerge—here, now—the control he'd gained in the last few years dissolving in the face of Cassie, all vulnerability and openness, standing right in front of him. It had been a relief when Ben emerged from the house. After that, he knew he couldn't stay.

CASSIE WAS UNSETTLED ALL AFTERNOON. Eventually, she decided to snuggle down somewhere warm and read her book. She turned on the heater in her bedroom. The burning dust from its summer season of disuse gave the air an acrid smell and set her on a hunt for a tealight candle for her fragrant oil burner. There were none left in her desk drawer.

"Dad!"

"Don't yell from your room!" he yelled from his office. She thumped across the floorboards and pushed his door wide. "What is it, Cas?"

"Do we have any more tealight candles?"

He frowned, distracted by his screen. "I dunno. Why don't you check Mum's drawers?" He waved behind him at the other desk.

Cassie opened the top drawer. There were no candles, just a messy assortment of staples and pens and paperclips.

The second drawer was full of manilla folders. She tried the bottom drawer. Bingo! A packet of candles was nestled neatly against a folded silk scarf, three tall taper candles, and a bronze candle snuffer. She lifted out the box and was about to close the drawer when a glint of silver caught her eye. It was a buckle. She tugged at it. It was attached to something. She pulled at it, and found herself lifting out a black, velvet-covered book, large enough that it had filled the bottom of the drawer. She glanced at Dad, but he was still intent on his work and didn't turn around. Shoving everything else back into place, she grabbed the box and the book, closed the drawer, and hurried out of the room.

"Did you find any?" Dad called out.

"Yep. All good!"

She eased her bedroom door quietly shut and plonked onto her bed to get a look at this strange new book in her hands.

It took only a moment of examination to realise that what she'd thought was a buckle was actually a lock. Why on earth would her mother have a locked book in the bottom of her desk drawer, for all the world as though it had been deliberately hidden? What could be so secret or important that Lyra felt she couldn't trust even her or Dad? Her stomach felt squirmy at the thought that there was anything Mum would want to hide from her, but churned even more at the feeling that she was betraying her somehow by even knowing of the book's existence.

She turned it over in her hands. It was almost an inch thick and had a velvet front cover embroidered with a silvery spider web pattern that shimmered in the light as she tilted the book. The black binding seemed thinner in some patches than others, as though much handling had worn it away. The pages, from what she could tell of them, were a coffee colour and the edges irregular, as though the paper was handmade. There looked to be a black ribbon folded inside the book, marking a page about three quarters of the way in. There was nothing on the back or spine to indicate what the book might be about. Perhaps it was a journal? Or a scrapbook? But if so, it must be a very old one, and clearly not something that Mum wrote in regularly, or surely Cassie would have seen it at some point.

Perhaps she should ask Dad. Yet the fact that she'd taken it from what was clearly a hiding place made her think that this might not be the best idea. And there was something else about the book, some feeling emanating from it that told her, if she allowed herself to believe it, that this was not Dad's business. Or the business of any man. It felt, not feminine exactly, but something belonging more to the moon than the sun, the night than the day. And somehow, Dad was the very daylight itself. She could replace it in the drawer before Mum returned. But before that, she needed to find the key.

CASSIE HAD WANTED to bring the book outside with her the next day, but it hadn't felt right, so she'd tucked it under her bed where it looked like a black cat in the shadow. She lay out on the grass in the afternoon sunshine. She'd been picking borage flowers for their salad and now lay twirling the delicate blue stars in her fingers with sunlight streaming through them, fancying she could see the individual cells that made up their glowing petals.

Dad was carving his wood—she could hear the gentle tapping of his mallet on his chisel. It was a satisfying sound, the kind of sound she could almost taste; something of home and comfort. There was no wind, the air was fresh, and the sun was warm on her skin. Only the bees seemed in a hurry to gather as much as they could before the cold arrived. She closed her eyes. The hypnotic golden patterns behind her eyelids, the sound of Dad's carving, and the humming of the bees lulled her into a state of blissful drowsiness...

She awoke with a start. The sun was hidden behind a broad bank of slate-grey clouds and the grass was damp and cold. She shivered and sat up. Her body felt achy, as though she'd been asleep awhile. There was no sign of Dad. Why hadn't he woken her up? She reached for her basket and accidentally tipped it over. Blue borage stars sprinkled the grass.

She felt it before she saw it. Something by the gate. Watching her. Without thinking, she reached out, grabbed a handful of the borage flowers and scattered them in a circle around herself. Only once the circle was complete did she stand up and turn to face the gate.

A huge black dog was staring at her, its eyes dark. She was sure it was taller than was natural, and its mouth was half open and panting, revealing large white canines. The small hairs on the back of Cassie's neck prickled, but she couldn't look away. For several long seconds, they stared at one another and neither of them moved. Then it stamped its front paws, lifted its head, gave a short howl, and turned tail in a strange, galloping run towards the forest.

Cassie stood in the ring of flowers long after the dog had gone, even as the clouds knitted themselves together above her and started spitting rain. It wasn't fear that kept her there, but frustration; there was something, something at the edge of knowing that was tugging at her. Something she should already know. If she moved, she would lose it for good. She stared into the forest as though that great black animal had carried off with it a secret about herself.

It was only when the rain began soaking through her

shirt and her toes felt numb that she finally surrendered, regathered the flowers, piling them into her pockets and headed inside, pushing open the front door with her wet basket.

She turned the hall lamp on. Where was Dad? She couldn't locate herself properly in time. The wall clock in the kitchen told her it was a little past three o'clock. Why was it so dark?

She ran upstairs.

"Dad?"

There was no answer. She pushed open the door to his office. He wasn't there. Her parents' bedroom? Not there either.

"Dad?!"

She raced from room to room, ran out into the tiny front garden through their barely-used front door, around past the car, still in its parking spot by the side of the house, and into the back garden. His wood sculpture had a rough face now. She shivered. It might have been a deer, or a kangaroo, but it also looked remarkably like the face of a hound. The mallet and chisel were lying on the ground as though they'd been dropped in a hurry. Dad was meticulous with his tools; it was not like him to leave them out, particularly in the rain. She gathered them up with shaking hands and placed them on the porch out of the weather, arranging them neatly in line with the boards, taking deep breaths to steady the racing, pounding feeling of her heart.

She re-entered the house. It felt cold, and there was a smell. She couldn't quite put her finger on it. It was a pungent, burnt smell. She ran again from room to room, checking the heater, the candles, the oil burner, the stove; then, in panic, ran to her bedroom and looked under her bed.

The book was still there, like a sleeping creature in the corner. She reached under and dragged it out.

"Dad, where are you?"

She stroked the book as though it really was the cat in the shadows she'd imagined and hugged it to her, trying to still the panic that was building inside her. Dad had just gone out to the shops or something. Maybe he hadn't wanted to disturb her sleeping in the garden. He must have walked. Yes, that was it. He'd be back soon. She decided to wait. She curled up on the bed with the book in her arms, closed her eyes and tried not to hear the rain lashing the roof and the rumbles of thunder overhead. Eventually she fell asleep, and her dreams were full of howling and the calling of ravens.

CASSIE WAS BEING SHAKEN AWAKE. She started and sat up, her heart kicking inside her like a wild horse. Her eyes must have looked wild too, because Ali was looking down at her with an expression full of concern.

"It's okay Cassie, you're all right."

Cassie stared around. The light in the room was grainy. Was it twilight? Morning? She couldn't work it out.

"Ali? What time is it?" Cassie tried to focus on Ali's face in the gloom.

"It's dusk."

"The smell." Cassie sniffed the air. "It's gone. Did you smell it?"

Ali looked confused.

"Something was burning." Then she inhaled sharply as she remembered. "Where's Dad?"

Ali shook her head. "Cassie, I'm sorry I don't know."

A wave of hot panic welled up in Cassie's stomach. "Maybe something's wrong with Mum!"

"Why don't we call your dad? Do you have a phone?"

Cassie shook her head. "Mum and Dad are anti-screen, for me anyway, not for them. Don't you have one?"

"I left mine at the cabin. I was just out for a walk. Your front door was open, and the lights were all off, so I thought I should check if everything was all right. We can walk back to my place and call from there if you'd like."

Some of the heat was dissipating, leaving Cassie's forehead damp with sweat. She wiped her face with the back of her hand. "Yes, I'd like that. Thank you."

"What's this?" Ali picked up the book that lay forgotten on the bed next to Cassie and frowned curiously at it.

Cassie reached for it and Ali placed it back in her hands.

"It's Mum's." She hugged it to her again.

Ali gave her a long look. "Do you know what it is?"

"No." Cassie stroked the velvet and touched her finger to the silvery web embroidery. "I mean, it's got a lock." She couldn't help the flush that spread across her cheeks as she avoided Ali's gaze.

"Did your mother mean for you to have it?"

Cassie shook her head. "Probably not. I mean, not really." And yet...She met Ali's eyes that looked grey and grave in this light. "She wouldn't mind me looking after it."

Ali seemed to be considering something.

"All right," she said eventually. "But I don't think you should bring it with you."

Cassie nodded and stashed the book back under the bed.

"Okay. Let's write a note for your dad, just in case he comes back first, shall we?"

≈

THE SILHOUETTES of the trees were like lace against the pink sky. Cassie was relieved they weren't entering the forest; the memory of the black dog was too near at hand. She followed Ali up Pardalote Lane and down a street that led towards the river. From here they took a trail that wound along the forest edge in the opposite direction to the swimming hole and the Walcotts' manor.

The evening was still and clear after the rain. Cassie drew in a long breath through her nose, trying to fill her lungs with the fresh peppermint smell of the eucalypts. Little bats fluttered across the path above them, one circling so close she could feel a shift in the air against her cheek, and she thought she might just have heard a clicking buzz in her ear as the tiny creature passed by. Or maybe she had just imagined the sound, the way she'd imagined fairies as a small kid. Dad had made her a bat detector once from a kit he'd bought at an electronics store. She had delighted in the discovery of their clicks and whirs filling a night silent to human ears. What other things were out there to be revealed that could not be seen, heard or understood by human senses? She also remembered a kind of sadness as she watched the staccato patterns on the screen, their jagged bounces matching those in her ears, knowing she could never experience this language directly, as a bat did, nor see what a bat could see.

"How're you going, Cassie? All right?" Ali had slowed down for her.

Cassie nodded in the blackness.

"Come on, we're almost there."

Just as they rounded a curve in the path where the first streetlights kicked in, a shape detached itself from the shadows in front of them. Cassie jumped. But surely that was too small to be a dog? Ali bent down.

"Hello, Fisket."

A skinny tabby cat with white under its chin had run up to Ali and was now rubbing itself against her legs as she patted it.

Ali looked up at Cassie, smiling. "He's the caravan park cat. A mouser I guess."

"They shouldn't keep it outside. It'll eat all the birds and things."

"You're right. I'm sure Fisket eats a lot more than mice." Ali straightened. "No birds tonight, all right?" she said seriously to the cat. Fisket seemed to consider and then began trotting ahead as if to show them how very well behaved he could be.

Cassie harrumphed, and followed the pair as they rounded the gates into the caravan park.

"Perhaps I can talk to the owners," whispered Ali, as though the cat could hear her. "Come on, my cabin is this way."

Fisket wandered off towards a cosy looking house, lit up from inside, that sat alongside the reception area and evidently belonged to the park's owners. Ali led them off to the right, to a small cabin at the back of the park alongside the river. Cassie could hear the white trickle of water over what sounded like a shallow, rocky section of the stream, and could just make out the tall shapes of tree ferns by the water's edge.

"Nice spot!"

"It's pretty, isn't it? Easier to tell in the day. Come on in." Ali turned the key in the lock and switched the porch light on so that Cassie could make her way up the wooden steps.

Ali's cabin looked more like a proper home than Cassie had imagined. There were cushions on the couches and a vase filled with a leafy bouquet on her kitchen bench. There were also clothes lying flung out on the bed, including the green jacket Cassie had so admired from Ali's photo.

"D'you like hot chocolate?" Ali was bobbing down, searching the fridge. She emerged with a block of chocolate in one hand and a carton of oat milk in the other.

"Yes, yum."

Ali pulled out a saucepan and cracked blocks of the chocolate into the pan, poured in the milk and lit the stovetop.

"Right," she said, wiping her hands on a tea-towel. "Now make yourself at home while I look for my phone."

She gathered some papers that had been spread out across the couch, arranged them neatly and placed them atop the pile of old-looking tourist guides and magazines stacked on a side-table. Then she slid a hand between the couch cushions.

"Aha! Here it is!"

Cassie flung herself down next to Ali. "Let's call him!"

They dialled Ben's number. There was a long silence as it rang out. They tried again, and once more, but Cassie's dad did not answer.

Cassie curled up her knees and hugged them to her chest.

"I'm sorry. Let's try again later, shall we?"

Cassie nodded.

Ali stood up quickly. "Oh, my goodness, the hot chocolate!"

She got to the stove just as the milk was frothing up to the edges of the pan.

When Ali brought her over a steaming mug, Cassie took its warmth into her hands and brought it to her cheek. It smelt delicious. This, at least, was something.

53

7

---

*C*assie was dozing on the couch while Ali made up a bed for her in the second bedroom when there came an urgent banging on the cabin door.

Her heart thundered with the sudden disturbance. "Ali!"

Ali raced into the room, blanket in hand. The banging came again, urgent and loud. She handed the blanket to Cassie, flicked up a section of blind near the door and peered through. Her shoulders loosened.

"It's okay," she said, and slid the chain from its latch.

The door opened wide, and someone tall and dark-haired burst into the cabin.

Cassie stared. "Julian!"

Julian's eyes widened.

"*Julian?*" Ali looked from one to the other, her eyebrows raised. "*The* Julian? Your friend?"

Cassie nodded numbly.

Julian's cheeks darkened. "Hi Cas."

"What are you doing here?"

Instead of answering her, Julian turned to Ali. "Can we

talk?"

Ali leaned her head to one side and eyed them both gravely. "Yes. But you can say what you need to in front of Cassie."

The irritation Cassie had felt spark up in him the last time they'd spoken arced across his face. Something soft and childlike inside her felt like curling up into a ball. She cradled the blanket to her chest and crossed her arms.

Julian began pacing the small room. He'd grown so much taller and broader since they'd last spent any proper time together. She wondered if he was comfortable in this new version of himself. It would take some getting used to; she doubted she could beat him in an arm wrestle now.

"I have some information. I came as soon as I could."

"It's all right, you really are free to speak." Ali pulled out a chair for Julian and perched herself on the couch next to Cassie.

Julian's gaze flickered to Cassie and back to Ali. "I found him."

Ali straightened and leaned forwards. "Go on."

Julian's eyes were wide; she'd never seen such intensity in his face before.

"It was the cockatoo that gave it away. The owner was out, and she was baiting me. I followed the trail as far as it went. I'd lost it before, at the same spot, just out the front of that house. But this time she was outside, screeching at me from her perch. I went for her. Just to make her be quiet. But as I launched and grabbed her tail, she shrieked: *Begone!* at me, and I was knocked down the steps by something I couldn't see. It was like a sharp blast of wind, or a fist to the guts."

Ali looked thoughtful. "That certainly points to her owner, doesn't it?"

"Are you talking about that plumber guy with the cockatoo? Did you hurt Bird?" Cassie glowered at Julian.

They both looked at her with surprise, as though they'd forgotten she was there.

"Yes, that's the one," said Ali softly. "But Bird's okay, isn't she Julian?"

The strange, twisted look on Julian's face indicated he wanted to say otherwise, but he nodded.

"Why'd you want to hurt her?"

Julian seemed so changed. He'd shown no unkindness towards an animal of any sort before. She remembered the gentle way he'd held her baby rabbits, his insistence that they not squash the mosquitoes that bit them in her garden. The harshness of his words, his face now, brought a painful feeling to her chest.

Ali sighed. "Okay, thanks for letting me know." She turned to Cassie. "It's getting late. We should all get some sleep."

Cassie stood up, the blanket falling to her feet. "No. Julian's not leaving until you two tell me what's going on!" She surprised even herself with how loud her voice sounded.

"It's not your business to worry about Cas," said Julian quietly. There was a heaviness in his voice that stopped Cassie short.

"What do you mean?"

He looked at her only briefly, then stared down at his hands that were twisting around each other like snakes.

Ali stood up as well. "He really should go, Cassie. We need to try and get hold of your dad again, remember?"

Cassie stomped, immediately recognising how infantile the gesture must seem to them. She needed to let this energy out, funnel the frustration into something.

Julian hurried to stand too, his forehead suddenly knitted

in concern. "Where's your dad?"

"I don't know."

Cassie didn't miss the quick glance exchanged between them. And it liquified her frustration into a fury that made her wish she had claws like that cockatoo so she could scratch at their faces. She ran to the door, wrenched it open and ran out into the cold. She could only see a glimmer of the porch in the light granted to her by the sliver of moon, but it was enough. She raced down the steps, back up the path past the now unlit house and out through the gates of the caravan park. They were calling her name. But it didn't matter. Nobody cared about her, no one. She was alone. They could keep their stupid secrets and their superiority. She didn't need them. She was fine on her own.

She ran until she could no longer hear their voices and then ran some more. The river rushed alongside her. She could hear it, leaping and bounding over boulders, diving into deep pools, through tangles of branches and bubbling under overhanging blackberry thickets. She and the river were going somewhere in this darkness together, and she was grateful for it.

Eventually, the moon slipped behind a cloud, and she could hardly see the path ahead of her. She stopped running. Had she come the right way? Had she missed the turnoff? It was so hard to tell. The night was like velvet, black on all sides, and all she could hear was the river.

The sweat on her forehead was cooling now that she was not moving, and her hands, toes, and the back of her neck were feeling cold. Had she been able to see, she was sure the water vapour in her breath would have been visible.

Continuing with the sound of the river to her left seemed the only sensible option. She was not going back to Ali and Julian. Their faces seemed to blossom out of the darkness at her. Her stomach squirmed. And she only now allowed herself to acknowledge the unaccustomed sensation. What was this feeling? Jealousy? It grew like a wave, as if to say, yes, yes, that is what I am, and she doubled over with the force of it. The path was gravelly and unyielding beneath her knees, but she could not keep walking. Everything melted into sadness, and she began to cry. It was Mum and Dad she wanted, here, now, holding her.

Her wailing melded into the voice of the river and her tears cooled quickly in the cold air. This was what it was to be left alone. A small voice in her mind, one that was removed from the rocking of her body and the loudness of her crying, observed that she had never really been lonely. She'd experienced solitude, yes, lots of it, and boredom too. But she'd never felt like this. She watched the path light up around her through blurry vision. The moon was emerging from its bank of clouds. She gazed at the shining boat sailing up and away from her, flawless and dispassionate.

A cracking sound to her left snapped her attention nearer at hand. Something large was moving through the bracken. She scrambled to her feet and fixed her eyes on the spot, holding her breath, her heart thumping. There was a rustle of leaves and she felt, rather than saw it emerge from the undergrowth, a moonlit glint on something huge and black. As it moved towards her, she could see it. First its face, the pools of its eyes and then the long, black body of the hound. When it was only a few metres from her, it stopped, lowered onto its haunches and sat, mouth open, gazing at her.

Running was not something she could have done, even had she thought it would have helped. She was frozen, impelled by the command of ancient DNA. *You must not run,* it said. Your ancestors didn't, and for this you exist. *Do not run.*

With only her eyes moving in her statue-like body, she watched the dog slowly rise and make its way towards her, its muzzle stretched out in a strange way as it slunk forward, almost as a human might creep towards a wild beast caught in a trap; one hand out in front, murmuring soothing words. Did she seem a trapped wild beast to this creature? She was shaking by the time the dog reached her. It was tall, up to her waist. It lowered its muzzle and began sniffing at her. She did not move. It pushed its nose gently under her hand, nudging her and then looking up at her as if to measure the effect of its encouragement.

"You want me to pat you?" Her voice was a shaky whisper.

She allowed her palm to come to rest between the dog's ears and gave it a tentative scratch. Its fur was deep and thick. It leaned into her and pushed up under her hand as she moved her fingers across its thick, silky coat. Then it stood up, making Cassie jump, moved a pace from her and turned around. She could see its white teeth reflecting in the moon-light, and its panting tongue. It loped along the track for a bit, then stopped. She took a step towards it, and once again it moved ahead and then paused, looking back as though waiting for her to catch up.

"Should I follow you?"

The dog half-leapt, its front paws thundering down like a small horse's.

"I guess that's a yes."

It let out a single bark.

"Okay. Lead on then."

Cassie's fear drained away as she followed the dog down the track. Finally, they reached the familiar streetlight at the end of Pardalote Lane. The dog led her up to her gate where it stopped, sat and stared at her.

"I see. You want me to go home."

Her house was still dark. She walked up the path. Rang her doorbell, knocked, and called out. But there was no answer. She knew Dad wasn't there. It felt empty.

She made her way back to the gate and the dog, who was sitting, watching her.

"I don't have a key. It's back with Ali."

The dog seemed to understand and stood up. She almost heard it say, *"Come on then"*, as it turned to continue down the path towards the forest. She followed. What else was there to do? Where else to go?

The moon remained obligingly bright, lacing the pathway with shadows as they entered under the trees. Eventually, they reached the bridge. She'd never crossed it at night before. The dog seemed confident ahead of her as she picked her way across the boards, thanking the moon for its light.

Cassie could tell they'd reached the edge of Julian's property by the dense silhouettes of the old rhododendrons and the soft turf beneath the soles of her shoes. She made her way forward until she could see the peaks and turrets of the Walcott's home, and one window up the top illuminated by a soft, yellow glow.

She'd lost sight of the dog in amongst the shrubs and maples. Now what? Should she ask Mr Walcott for a bed for the night? She was wishing she'd stayed with Ali; how ridiculously childish of her to have run away.

She rounded another shrub and recognised the small, sheltered glade, like a fairy ring beneath a huge conifer, surrounded by azaleas and rhododendrons, that was the place that she, Julian, and his mother had met for so many picnics and stories. She sank to her knees on the soft moss and pine needles, her ribcage a hollow ache for Violeta.

It was a moment before she realised she was not alone.

Just on the other side of the glade, as though a part of the dense shadow, there was someone standing, turned away from her. All she could see was the illuminated planes and shadows of their back. Cassie drew in a sharp breath. A young man with a tangle of dark hair turned to her, his face a shade lighter in the moonlight than under the sun.

"Julian?"

"Cassie."

They made their way towards one another in the dark. In the middle of the glade, he reached and pulled her towards him. She could feel heat radiating from him in the cold air. Blood rushed to her cheeks. Julian had become stronger. She shook free of his hands, confused by the electric feeling shimmering across her skin.

"Are you angry with me?" he asked, his voice a low whisper.

She met his eyes, luminous in her memory, now like portals into the night.

"Yes." It was all she could say. Nothing made sense anymore. Nothing.

"I'm sorry," he said.

She shivered.

"You're cold."

"No. I'm not. You're the crazy one out here wearing a t-shirt."

He looked down at his bare arms as though surprised. Then he laughed. And she wanted to cry because she hadn't heard that sound for so long.

"What's happening, Julian?"

He reached out for her again, and this time she allowed him to take her hand. She felt a charge run through her where their fingers touched, and as though a switch had flicked inside her, she needed to be closer still, to drink in this new, primed feeling. He drew her against him, brought her hand to his heart, and she could hear his breathing, feel his heartbeat kicking wildly beneath her palm. This sparking heat, this scent of earth and pine; it was everything she wanted—

"Cassie!" A voice called out from the forest edge, wild with worry."Cassie! Where are you? Cassie!"

Cassie flinched. "It's Ali."

For a moment, Julian didn't move, his chest rising and falling beneath her hand. But when Cassie stepped back, he was swiftly at her side.

"Yes, let's go."

They found Ali by the bridge. She rushed forward and pulled Cassie into her arms.

"I was so worried!"

Cassie hugged her back. "I'm sorry."

"Come," Ali said, tugging at her hand and leading them back across the bridge. "We have to hurry."

"What is it?" Julian asked her.

"He's done it. You were right. If we get there quickly, we might still have a chance."

Cassie followed them, the spark of Julian's touch doused by a new wave of exasperation.

They ran through the night, back along the forest path that was even brighter now that the moon had risen higher in the sky. Then, to Cassie's surprise, Ali led them down the little track that led to the swimming hole.

"What are we doing here?" she asked.

"It's the deepest pool in the river," Ali was still talking to Julian. "I felt it as I ran past."

Julian nodded, took a few steps towards the water's edge, and peered out over it. Cassie frowned. Then she saw it: just a shimmer of something above the water, as though the river had an extra layer of liquid made of light flowing across its surface.

"What is that?"

Julian looked at her in surprise and followed her gaze out over the water.

"Should she be able to see that?" Julian asked Ali.

Ali cocked her head to one side, her silver eyes examining Cassie in the moonlight.

"There's more to Cassie than you know, Julian."

Irritation abruptly replaced Cassie's wonderment. "Could you two please stop talking about me as though I'm not here?"

"Sorry," said Ali, taking her hand and leading her down to the water.

"Sorry," said Julian, but with a renewed note of something guarded, wary, in his voice.

They all stared out across the water. Cassie had so many questions, but the grave silence of her companions stilled them for now.

"I've only done this once before," whispered Ali.

"One more time than either of us," said Julian.

"Okay." She took a deep breath and turned to Cassie. "Now don't freak out. We're all going to walk into the water, and I just need you to make sure you keep hold of both of us. No matter what happens. All right?"

Cassie shook her head. "Why on earth would we do that?"

"Please. I just need you to trust me. Do you think you could?"

Cassie met her eyes. "All right. Yes. But, just so you know, I *am* freaking out."

Ali nodded. "Totally understandable. But we really have to do this rather quickly."

They formed a ring, each taking the other's hand—Ali on

Cassie's left and Julian on her right—and shuffled awkwardly into the freezing water. Cassie tried not to think about what they were doing—because what they were doing was clearly pure insanity. As they drew closer to the shimmering layer, the water became warmer until it was almost hot. Her eyes widened, and she tightened her grip on them both.

"Keep holding tight," ordered Ali.

Cassie nodded.

"No matter what," said Ali again firmly.

The next instant Cassie was screaming, until her head went under, and then she was gasping at the surface for breath. She managed one lungful of air before being fully submerged, her legs flailing about in deep water. Ali's hand was no longer gripping hers; Cassie was holding onto what felt like a piece of rubbery kelp. And Julian's hand seemed to have turned to sandpaper, with sharp points digging into her palm.

No matter what! She didn't know if it was her own voice screaming in her head or Ali's, but she gripped these strange, twisting things and did not let go.

She needed to breathe. She kicked and pulled at her weighted arms, writhing with panic. Then, as though she'd been tumbled by an enormous wave, she was pushed into a somersault, and it was impossible to tell up from down. She did the only thing she could and held tight. But she had to breathe. Now! With her eyes squeezed shut and lungs burning, she tried to push herself towards what she hoped was the surface. But she was being pulled down by the seaweed and the claws in her hands. A dizzy blackness overwhelmed her, and she couldn't hold on anymore. This was it. She was done.

8

---

*S*omeone's lips were on hers, then a terrifying weight on her chest. She thrashed and pushed until she was released from it. Her body spasmed and a jet of water forced its way out of her mouth. She coughed and retched until it was all gone.

It was a long while before she could open her eyes. The first thing she saw was a purple sky, the purple of lavender. She shut her eyes again. The next time she opened them, Julian was looking down at her, cold drops of water from his hair falling on her face. For a moment, he was her sky. He took her hand and squeezed it gently.

"Cas? Cassie?"

She blinked and slowly pulled herself up to sitting.

"Oh, thank goodness!" Ali crouched next to Julian, her eyes wide and her face bloodless.

Cassie tried to swallow. Her throat felt raw. It was as though a stoking iron had scoured her insides. She folded her arms across her ribcage with the burning pain of it.

"She's cold!" said Julian. He wrapped his arms around her.

He felt warm and strong.

"Ali, how can we get her warm?"

"You're doing just fine, Julian. Stay with her. I'll be back with you both in a minute. Hold on, Cassie, okay?"

Cassie tried to nod, but her eyelids were closing again. She leaned into Julian's heat, breathing in the scent of his skin.

Within minutes, Ali was back. Cassie got to her feet, grateful for Julian's supporting arm beneath her elbow. It took a moment for the world to stop spinning.

"Thank you, I'm good now."

He let go and stepped back.

Ali's expression was scrutinising, concerned. "Can you walk?"

Every muscle in her body ached, and all she wanted to do was sleep, but she nodded. "I think so."

It took Cassie a moment to register that it was no longer dark. Had she been out of it for longer than she'd thought? Or were they somewhere where it was not night? A chill spread through her. She couldn't quite face either of those possibilities. She looked down at her feet in their water-logged gym boots. Beneath them was soft grass, a turf similar to the natural lawns she'd seen in national parks where kangaroos and wallabies grazed. Next to them was water, the water she'd almost drowned in. How long ago? She realised she could hear no trickling sounds; the water was not a flowing river: it was a still, glassy pool, its surface a lilac tint. She looked up. The sky really *was* purple.

"You sure you're okay to walk?" Julian was watching her.

His clothes were dry. How were hers still wet?

"How d'you do that?"

He frowned. "Do what?"

Ali, who was already walking ahead, turned back to them.

"Come on, we should move." Then she raised her eyebrows. "Oh Cassie, sorry!"

She made her way back to Cassie's side.

"Close your eyes."

"What? Why?"

Ali placed her hand gently over Cassie's eyes and she felt a warm tingle like a golden wave from her shoulders to her toes.

"There."

She looked down, patted her clothes. "They're dry!"

Ali's expression suddenly fitted her pixie hair perfectly. "Okay, let's go."

"Where're we heading?" asked Julian.

"It's just a bubble," said Ali. She sounded disappointed. Cassie thought she detected a note of something else in her voice too—longing, sadness?

"Meaning?"

"Meaning he wasn't, or isn't yet, strong enough to punch a hole all the way through, so to speak. Or perhaps he didn't want to. He might use this merely as a convenient mode of transport."

Julian nodded, as though this made sense to him.

Cassie followed them, her mind already too full of strangeness to add anything new to its confused tangles.

They were walking through a forest with trees like none she'd ever seen. Their trunks were white, like the manna gums along the river at home, but three times the size. She looked up. The canopy towered over them from a dizzying height, and it reminded her of those huge rainforest trees she'd seen once in a documentary about Borneo. Ali led them along a tiny, winding track through a sea of low ferns. Colourful things flitted around them, never staying still enough for Cassie to get a proper glimpse of what they were.

The more they walked, the more she thought she heard a kind of humming or a song that moved through the forest in waves, as though in place of a breeze; the trees were singing to each other. The way the sunlight angled through the forest made her think it must be early morning, or maybe late afternoon. She wasn't sure.

Julian looked back at her, a soft smile on his face. He reached for her hand, their palms touched, and a thrill jolted through her. It was a dream. Surely? Her whole being was alive. She felt she must actually be glowing with the energy of this magical place.

Julian raised his free hand and drew something in the air with his index finger. As though he'd drawn it with a pen, a golden 'C' shimmered in the air before falling away. Heat rushed to her cheeks. She tried it too. Her 'J' held for a moment and then dispersed back into the surrounding air.

Ali was ahead, leading them hurriedly along the track, seemingly oblivious to the magic around them. Cassie was aware of the light dimming as they walked. Or was it that the forest was getting thicker around her, with more shrubs and taller ferns, and twisted branches dripping with moss? The air was cooler now too.

They crossed a small stone bridge over a clear stream, and as she stepped onto the muddy ground on the other side, a ring of colourful fungi around her shoe startled her. As she lifted her foot, they vanished. It happened again with the next step, and the next: tiny forests of shining mushrooms of all shapes and sizes popping up where she walked. They appeared and disappeared as though she was some warped version of Persephone bringing forth the spring flowers with her footprints upon the earth.

In her fascination with the fungi, she hadn't realised quite how dark the tangled forest around her had become. The fungi in the mud now seemed to glow. Soon they were the only source of light, and it was difficult to see the path ahead.

"Julian? Ali?" she called ahead into the silence. "Are you still there?"

"Yes!" Ali's voice was fainter than Cassie had expected. Was she really that far behind them both? She shivered.

"I'm here, Cas." Julian's voice was much closer. With relief, she saw him loom out of the shadows in front of her. His face was lit by a green, glowing plate fungus on a tree next to them, making his eyes seem to glitter. Then she realised his whole face was glimmering, as though lit from within by a thousand tiny fairy lights.

His eyes widened. "You're glowing!" he said.

She brought her hands up in front of her; sure enough, they too were luminous in the blackness. They both stretched their arms out, watching the dance of light across their skin. Cassie moved her fingers, swishing them around, making patterns like birthday cake sparklers.

"Julian! Cassie!" Ali's voice was closer now. Cassie squinted through the dark, but it was hard to see through the glow coming off her own face. Something shining appeared behind Julian. It was Ali. "I don't like this. Let's all stay close, so we don't lose each other. I'll keep us on the track."

"How much further do you think?" Julian's voice was measured, but Cassie knew him well enough to hear the tinge of fear in his words.

Ali's glimmering face, somehow perfectly right with her silver eyes, shook from side to side.

"Honestly, I don't know. Just hold tight."

The singing sighing of the trees was gone, replaced by a solid silence. Every sound they made seemed amplified and Cassie tried not to think about what might be in the forest on either side of them, hearing them, watching their shimmering passage through the dark. Suddenly, being lumines-cent didn't seem quite so much fun. She breathed in and out, trying to steady herself, her stomach clenching.

After an interminable time placing one foot in front of the other, the colours of the glowing fungi at her feet whirling like a kaleidoscope against the darkness, they stopped.

"Here it is. The Weaver Gate," said Ali.

"Have you ever been through one like this before?"

"No." Ali's voice was small and thin.

Cassie felt a prickle of fear.

"It's what we came for." Julian's voice retained an under-current of wariness, but he sounded resolute all the same.

Something soft brushed Cassie's face. She squealed. The others turned their shimmering faces towards her.

"What is it?" asked Ali.

"I don't know." Cassie was glad of the darkness as she felt her cheeks turn hot. Childish, always so childish.

Ali and Julian looked at one another. Cassie took a step back. It was as though a spotlight was shining on them and Cassie was receding into the night.

Ali was an exquisite, wondrous creature. Wide, luminous eyes, a perfect rose petal of a mouth. And Julian, in this moment, seemed a tall, shining god. She was struck by the realisation that he was no longer a boy; not at all. But she still felt like a girl, lost and out of place with these two other-worldly beings.

A pair of hands came to rest lightly on her shoulders. They were soft and cold. She jumped. And then she froze. They were not Julian's, or Ali's; both of whom had turned to examine the shining thing in front of them, the Weaver Gate, or whatever it was. She suppressed the scream trying to force its way out of her. A voice whispered in her ear.

"Yes, they are beautiful. See how they lean towards one another. They understand each other. Not like you, child. You are nothing like them. Nothing to them. Not important. You're just baggage they couldn't rid themselves of because they had to babysit you. Little one, come away from them. They'll only hurt you."

Cassie sucked in a breath, cold with fear. She couldn't move or cry out now, even if she'd wanted to. The hands tightened on her.

"Do you think he'll really want you? Don't delude yourself, child. He wants her, not you. Come away. Come with someone who will cherish you like a queen. Come. Follow me."

The hands lifted from her, and she felt herself pivoting on the spot, spun like a magnet. A glowing ball of light was hovering above the track, slowly making its way back the way they'd come. It was a glorious thing. And it wanted her. It was warm and good, and it would care for her. She took a step towards it.

"Yes." The voice breathed like a caress, causing a hot spark to travel down her body. Her eyes widened, her skin tingled, and she moved towards it, an ecstatic energy fizzing up and down her spine, coursing through her.

"Come, come away." The voice was rich and deep now. She wanted to be in it, surrounded by it, held by that glow. It would satisfy her in every way: parent, friend, lover. She would meld with it, become it, and she would feel peace.

"Cassie! No!" A harsh voice ripped into her.

Something hit her chest and she let out a *whoomph* of air and fell to the ground, winded, unable to scream out. There was a dark shape above her, pinning her on all sides, hot breath in her face, two heavy weights on her chest. She screwed up her eyes and tried to hit out, writhing and kicking, panic replacing the euphoria of only moments before.

Someone was gripping her wrists now and restraining her legs with their knees.

"Cas! Stop, it's me!" It was Julian's voice from above her. He was holding her down.

She stopped thrashing. "Julian?"

"Yes, it's me, just me." He hugged her to him, and she heard him release a shaky breath.

"I don't understand." She pressed her hands to her temples. "I don't understand any of this."

He held her close, and for a moment she allowed herself to just breathe, breathe him in, his scent of sun-warmed rocks and the lingering trace of pine needles. His voice vibrated in his chest against her ear. "It's all right now. It's all right."

She'd wandered quite a long way back along the track. The light that had led her here seemed to have vanished. She shivered. It had felt so good, so right. But whatever it was that had seduced her away from her friends into the pitch-black depths of the forest of an unknown world had suddenly lost its potency.

This time, she held tight to Julian's hand as he led them steadily back to Ali's faint glow.

"Quick!" Ali said as they reached her. "I can't hold it for much longer."

Ali had her arms above her head as though she were holding the bottom of a very heavy curtain, a cut-out piece of the night itself; black, with aurora-like light oscillating along its edges. In front of her was a square of something grey, billowing and curling like smoke trapped in glass. A sense of dread filled Cassie as she watched it, mesmerised.

"Go through, now!"

Julian strode forward, and before she could protest, he pulled her across the threshold behind him.

9

*C*assie coughed and spluttered, trying to expel the hot, sweet tang of smoke from her nose and lungs. The back of her throat was dry and burning.

Ali crawled up to her, coughing too, and patted Cassie on the back. "Beats maths lessons though, don't you think?"

Cassie stared at Ali through streaming eyes. Then she began to laugh, in great, gulping bursts. Or was she crying? She wasn't sure, but the vibrations of her belly felt good.

"Shush, you two!" hissed Julian. "We have no idea where we are."

The air around them felt close, and the sound, muffled, as they dusted themselves off. As the smoke cleared, they could see that they were in a small room, bare of furniture, with a low, wooden, A-framed ceiling and one dirty window admitting a diffuse golden light. There was no sign of the strange portal they had arrived through.

Julian got to his feet and made his way silently to the window. They watched him wipe a patch of the glass clear of dust and peer out.

"Don't know if the sun's rising or setting, but I can see rooftops. Lots of them. And some taller buildings. A church, some high-rises."

"We're in a city?" Cassie whispered.

"Looks that way."

Ali took in the small space. "And I reckon this is an attic."

"Do you think it's his?" Julian's gaze darted around the room.

Ali's face grew serious. "It could be."

Julian stalked across to one of two doors leading from the room and opened it, revealing a small bathroom with a round skylight. Ali, her face drawn, leaned her head against the wall. Julian tried the second door.

"This one leads downstairs. Let's go."

"I'm not going anywhere," said Cassie, rubbing at the dull ache in her temples, "until you two tell me what's going on. And also, I'm exhausted."

Julian regarded her, and she was forcefully reminded of his father when he'd first assessed her all those years ago. His jaw moved sideways a fraction, and then he closed the door and pulled the latch across.

"That should keep whoever lives here out for a bit," he said.

"Unless they're a Weaver," said Ali, her voice weary.

"Which they probably are," said Julian.

Cassie could barely lift her head.

"So, are you going to tell me?"

"I think it's better if we all get a bit of sleep first." Ali looked out at the darkening sky. "Julian, are you happy to keep first watch? Wake me in an hour?"

"Yes, of course," he said.

Julian looked grim as he settled himself cross-legged next to Ali. It felt strange to Cassie that she couldn't read the nuances of his face. They had once been so familiar. Were these new emotions, new expressions shadowing his features? Or had he just never felt these things around her before? Was he frustrated now? Impatient? Angry? He turned away. She was sure he'd noticed her searching his face for understanding. A wave of bone-deep weariness washed through her, and she turned away too.

"Wake me when it's my turn," she said, before surrendering to the heavy hand of sleep.

IT WAS MUCH LONGER than a couple of hours before Cassie was shaken gently awake. Ali was looking down at her.

"Julian's asleep," she whispered.

Cassie sat up quickly. "What time is it?"

"I'm not sure, some time before dawn I think."

"Have you slept?"

"A little," she smiled and placed her slender hand over Cassie's. "It's okay, Julian and I took turns."

"You should have woken me!" Cassie felt her stomach clench. Did they think she was just a child who needed her rest?

"You've been through a lot, Cassie. I sleep little these days, anyway."

Cassie would have laid a bet that this wasn't true, but she tried to feel grateful. Julian was lying with his back to them, the rhythmic rise and fall of his breathing only just perceptible. It had been years since she'd seen him asleep. What other parts of his life had she not borne witness to in the time he'd been away?

Ali followed her eyes. "I'm sorry I didn't put it together

earlier that he was the friend you'd spoken to me about. He hadn't got around to telling me his name."

The time in Ali's cabin already seemed a lifetime ago. Remembering brought all the questions flooding back, but Cassie bit down on her bottom lip, sensing that if she remained quiet, Ali might say more.

"I'm sorry you got dragged into this."

Cassie's gaze travelled over Julian's still form. He looked younger, more like the boy she remembered.

"What exactly *is* it I've been dragged into?"

Ali sighed and rubbed at her temples. "Julian's part is not for me to tell. But I owe you some of my story."

Her eyes began darting about as if she were trying to find an escape route, then she blinked and turned her face to the pink light blossoming in the sky outside the window.

"I have an admission to make. I feel ashamed to tell you, Cassie, but I wasn't in your area by chance when your dad chose me to be your tutor." She hugged her arms around herself as though she were cold.

Cassie could hear her own heartbeat in her ears. "I don't understand. Aren't you a real tutor?"

"Oh yes, I have been for the last three years; it's just..."

Cassie waited for her to continue, hardly daring to breathe in the close silence around them.

"I've spent years. So long," Ali whispered finally. "I've done so much research, talked with anyone who claimed to know anything about the world between worlds. I've learnt a lot. But I still haven't found a way. This is the closest I've ever come."

"To what?"

Ali looked as though she was studying the dusty floor-boards, but when she lifted her gaze, Cassie was surprised to see a fierce fire in her eyes.

"To finding him."

"Who?" Cassie found herself whispering.

"His name was...is...Tomas."

Cassie didn't know what to say. She didn't know what she'd expected, but it hadn't been this.

"He was stolen away. And it was my fault. I need to find him, Cassie." Her voice was suddenly raw and bitter. "This is the first true portal I've found, and it didn't lead me there. It was just a bubble, nothing more than a passageway."

"Oh."

It was all Cassie could say. She wanted to say more, to say she was sorry for her, but nothing made sense. Ali's expression flickered like a lightning storm between frustration, yearning and self-loathing, until she stood up and crossed to the window. The rising sun lent her pale skin a golden sheen. She turned back to Cassie.

"I'm sorry. I allowed my selfish pursuit to put you in danger. The most important thing to do now is to get you home safe."

Cassie opened her mouth, closed it again. Julian rolled over. They both watched him, and then Cassie rose and joined Ali, staring with her out into the brilliant, blinding dawn.

"I'm not sure my home *is* safe now. I want to stay with you," she said. "We both have lost people to find."

BY THE TIME JULIAN AWOKE, Cassie's stomach was churning with hunger. They helped themselves to what they hoped was drinkable water from the bathroom tap, and splashed their faces clean.

With the sun high above the city skyline, they unlatched

the door and made their cautious way downstairs. Both the steps and the wooden railings were thick with dust that dampened their footsteps. The first landing opened out onto a corridor of closed doors, whose floor was splotched with patches of bird droppings and feathers. Above them was a row of dirty skylights, some with cracks and others with holes as though stones had been dropped through them. A couple of pigeons were tapping their way across the glass, and in another spot, just under a warped piece of wood with an opening above it to the sky, was a swallow's nest made of balled-up bits of mud.

"Looks well cared for," said Julian.

Cassie snorted.

Ali was already making her silent way down the second flight of stairs.

The next floor down had a similarly abandoned air.

"Must have been an old apartment block," said Cassie, the dust and cobwebs over the wood and cracking plaster quickly soaking up her words.

The next landing opened out into a wide, pink and grey marble mezzanine with steps leading down to a large, wooden-framed door whose glass panels were heavy with grime. Two large plane trees were visible outside the neglected front door. Some of their dry leaves had found their way in from the street, littering the terrazzo floor.

Julian crunched across the leaves and pulled at the door. It didn't budge. He heaved again.

"Locked."

Cassie's stomach growled.

Ali looked around. "He must have got in somehow."

"He's a Weaver. Couldn't he just magic his way in?" said Julian.

Ali scowled. "Of course not. It doesn't work like that."

"Who the heck *is* this Weaver guy?" said Cassie, more loudly and with more force than she'd intended. Her hunger was making her light-headed and irritable.

They both looked at her. A frown flickered briefly on Ali's face. "We don't strictly know he's a *he*."

"We don't?" asked Julian with surprise.

Ali shook her head. "Could be anyone with the power and will to tear the fabric between the worlds. Everything I know is only theory, mind you. But from what I've learnt, it's not your average Weaver or other magical citizen who has this amount of power and is willing to use it in this way. It's not" —she paused—"advised."

"*Don't try this at home* kind of thing?" said Cassie, trying to ignore the uneasy rolling of her stomach, which might have been hunger but was more likely due to the fact they were calmly discussing types of magical citizens as though they were flavours of salad dressing.

She laughed and heard her laughter echoing back at her from the smooth marble walls. It sounded slightly hysterical.

"You know, if I hadn't just followed you through that fairy forest, I would be running a mile from you right now."

Ali rubbed her forehead. "Perhaps you *should* be, Cassie. I'm..."

"Please don't say you're sorry again," Cassie interrupted. "Come on, let's just find a way out of here."

There was a bang as Julian brought his shoulder up against a door that looked as though it led to another lobby. They heard something crack, and he pulled the door wide with a flourish.

Instead of a lobby, they tumbled out into a laneway lined with bins. Ali picked up a broken stick lying by the door and examined it closely.

"This must have been wedged in to keep it open." She

placed the stick between the frame and the base of the door and pushed it carefully closed. "So we can come back if we need to."

"Just hopefully not at the same time as ye olde Weaver," said Julian.

"Indeed," said Ali.

Cassie looked back at the door, trying to find a detail about it she could commit to memory. It was wooden, with peeling dark blue paint. The only feature that differentiated it from the other back-alley doors was its unloved look. The handle, though, was an ageing bronze with something pressed into the metal. She stepped up to examine it. It was a pair of what looked like wolves following each other in an endless circle around the handle. A memory flashed into her mind: two black dogs in a golden clearing, weaving around one another as though they were dancing.

10

"I guess the question now"—said Julian, staring down the alleyway—"is, where *are* we?"

Ali narrowed her eyes. "And *when* are we?"

Cassie, who had been watching scudding clouds consume a thin band of sky between the tall buildings, brought her attention to the laneway. It looked normal enough, with walls covered by a bright layering of street art and cars parked in short, back-shop driveways. They seemed like standard cars, neither old nor futuristic. And there were definitely no horses, despite the black cobblestones that must once have rung with the iron clopping of hooves.

"Looks like a regular street to me," Ali said.

Julian was squinting through the window of the nearest car. "No worries about the *when!*" His voice carried easily across the quiet laneway. "No time travel, going by the model and odo reading."

Ali and Cassie stared at him.

He shrugged. "Unless the owner never drives anywhere; then we could be a year or so off."

"Unlikely," said Ali.

Cassie shook her head, laughing in disbelief. "How do you even *know* that?"

Julian gave her a pleased little smile and raised an eyebrow. "Just do."

Ali laughed, hooking her arm into Cassie's.

Julian's footsteps scraped loudly as he re-joined them, and Cassie shivered.

Ali suddenly tensed beside her. "Something's not right."

They followed Ali's gaze. A fog was rolling towards them, whiting out each line of the street's bluestone cobbles, consuming the bins, the cars and the graffiti like a fast-advancing army. Menacing. Unyielding.

"Run!" Ali tugged at Cassie's arm, pulling her out of her stunned inertia and racing ahead. "Come on, this way!"

Julian grabbed Cassie's hand, and they sped after Ali, the fog at their heels. Ali spun left, into a wider street and Cassie felt something icy lick the back of her legs, pulling her from Julian as he swung around the corner.

"Cassie!"

He reached back for her, but the cold twisted up her calves and past her knees and it felt like trying to run through water. She stretched, trying to grab his hand.

"Cassie!" His voice was thick with panic.

The cold fog was clamping around her hips now, her waist, her chest, pulling her in. She could feel its grip on her shoulders, closing over the back of her head, sighing into her ears. She tried to twist free, but like a fly trapped in honey, the more she flailed about, the more quickly she became engulfed, until it was up over her chin, her mouth. Now she couldn't even scream. Soon she wouldn't be able to breathe. Some instinct told her to stop struggling, to conserve what oxygen she had left. She pulled in a last, desperate breath through her nose and closed her eyes. With that, the sighing sound in her ears became an unearthly scream. Her heart beat wildly, terror forcing the blood into her limbs in one last futile attempt to break free.

There was a tearing sound, and someone's hands clasped around her wrists. She was being pulled forwards, her body dragged and ripped through the viscous fog. Julian's face crystallised out of the vapour. He was pulling her towards him, his arms and neck taut with strain. Her mouth was free. She could breathe again. Then her head and shoulders, waist and legs. Julian pulled her into the circle of his arms.

"The flowers!" someone was shouting.

It was Ali. Cassie thought she could make out her form in the thinning mist ahead of them.

"Cassie! Those blue ones. Do you have any left?"

She tried to decipher the riddle of Ali's words, staring desperately into Julian's face, the scream still ringing in her ears.

Julian raised his voice over the roar that was gathering like a tornado behind them. The fog, finding them again.

"In your pocket!" he yelled, holding her by her shoulders, his gaze drilling into her, willing her to understand.

"Oh!" The borage flowers. From a lifetime ago.

She felt an icy whip lick her leg again and plunged her hands into the pocket of her jeans. The fog caught hold of her ankle as her fingers closed over a handful of the petals, so delicate and withered that she could hardly feel them. As she drew out the crushed flowers, a bubble of clarity enveloped her. Time seemed to slow to allow her to do what she knew she must do. She sprinkled the flowers in a full circle around herself and Julian. He pulled her tight against him, and all around them was suddenly silent. She could hear only his uneven breathing and the feel of his chest expanding and contracting against hers. She closed her eyes, her head spinning.

Then the bubble around them burst. The roaring returned, but eased back to a sigh as the fog's icy grip loosened and slithered from around her ankle, its rolling, heaving mass retreating down the street, into the alleyway, receding from them as quickly as it had come.

Julian tensed, then quickly loosened his hold around her and stepped back. Cassie captured the fleeting furrowing of his brow and felt her heart shrink into a cold, hard rock in her chest. He didn't meet her gaze as Ali ran forward and embraced her.

"Well done! You did so well!" The relief in Ali's voice washed through Cassie.

She hugged her back fiercely, her tutor's slight frame like that of a child's in her arms compared with Julian's.

"What *was* that?" Cassie's entire body was trembling now.

Ali's eyes darted around, still wary. "I don't know. Some kind of trap, I'm guessing. Maybe meant to finish off anyone who used that Gate who isn't a Spiritweaver."

"A what?"

Julian's eyes narrowed, and he addressed Ali. "Alisa, we need to find somewhere safer."

Ali tilted her head to the side, considering. Then she pulled a bankcard out of her back pocket. "Well, I *am* hungry. And if we're in our own time period, this might actually be useable. So why not breakfast?" She looked up at the sky—a clear blue once more—trying to locate the position of the sun. "Or lunch."

"Fine. Let's try this way," said Julian, pointing down the lane.

They followed the small street until it opened out onto a broader, familiar one lined with trees, cafés and parked cars.

The incongruous normality of it struck Cassie. There were plenty of people here, some in neat, dark clothing with an air of purpose, grabbing bites to eat on short lunch breaks; others wandering in a more relaxed way, reading menus in restaurant windows, arm in arm, smiling, laughing. Everything completely normal. A sharp burn of hunger flashed through her stomach.

"Will here do?" she asked them, stopping in front of the nearest café.

Red-striped umbrellas shaded outside tables set between two large apple crates trailing lush greenery. They seated themselves at a corner table. The air was pleasantly warm and the conversations of diners inside the restaurant flowed out to them in a gentle hum. Cassie's eyelids felt heavy. She gazed at two sparrows stealing leftovers from an adjacent table as Ali asked the waiter for menus.

"Cas?"

Julian's deep voice startled her. Her eyes fluttered open. He was looking at her, no trace of anything hard in his expression now. She felt her cheeks warm.

"Sorry. So tired."

Ali laid a sympathetic hand over Cassie's. "Food will help."

Their food arrived with a glorious waft of scent that immediately set Cassie's mouth watering. The taste of butterscotch and toasted walnuts was, right at this moment, as magical as anything she'd experienced in the last twenty-four hours, or however long it had been.

She glanced at Ali and Julian, similarly focussed on their food. Ali's face still seemed to shimmer slightly, even under the shadow of the umbrellas. A dark green devil's ivy reached out from the planter behind her as though it wanted to caress her cheek. How could she not have seen this luminous otherworldliness when she first met her tutor? True, she'd found her beautiful, had liked the quirky way she dressed, but she could see now that there was something other about her, something magical. And Julian, whose inscrutable eyes had become a mystery to her; how was he caught up in this?

Suddenly, forcefully, all she wanted was her dad. The feeling was like a wave, and it pushed her back in her seat. Where was he? And why had he left her? Or had she been the one who had left? Who was this person sitting in Cassie's skin, speaking with her voice, who knew to arrange starflowers in a ring to ward off danger? That was the question whose answer frightened her the most; the dark place she truly feared to look. Ali knew, and Julian too. Clearly, they knew what she could do, better than she herself. The spirit in the forest that had so nearly led her astray seemed to speak in her ear. But this time it was her own voice. *You are nothing like them.* Had it spoken truly? What did Ali and Julian know that she did not? A thought struck her, and she breathed in sharply.

"How did you both know about the borage flowers?"

Her tone was more accusatory than she'd meant it to be. Yet, neither of them had been there when she'd been gathering the flowers. Neither of them had seen the dog, or the strange inclination that had overtaken her and directed her to cast that first protective circle. Had they been spying on her? She remembered the peace, the sunshine, the sound of her dad carving wood. A stab of anxiety flooded her again. Was he safe? Was he worried about her?

She watched them both staring at her and waited for one of them to say something. Ali had just taken a drink of orange juice and was eyeing Cassie over the rim. She lowered the glass and seemed about to speak when Julian interjected.

"I saw you, Cassie." There was tension in his face, his jaw taut.

"I came to check on you, to see if you were all right. I knew the Weaver had been to your place and—"

"How did you know?"

He glanced briefly at Ali. "Alisa told me."

Cassie's heart hammered, and blood rushed to her ears. She turned to Ali, who nodded seriously and opened her mouth again to speak, but Cassie cut across her.

"You were spying on me?" She hissed the question, wishing they weren't in a public place so that she could properly release the hot anger that was building up in her.

"No. It wasn't like that." He opened his mouth as though he wanted to say more and then closed it again.

She crossed her arms against her thumping chest. "What *was* it like then?"

Ali leaned forward. "Cassie, I know there's so much we haven't explained. I know it's confusing—"

Cassie pushed her chair back with a loud scrape, trembling with all the held-in energy, the anger, the disorientation. She stood up, needing to move, to shake everything out. The middle-aged couple who'd just taken the table next to them looked up from their menus with startled expressions. Cassie's face burned. It didn't matter. She needed to move, to run.

"Cassie!" Ali's voice was faint and far away, as though she was calling though a long tunnel.

Cassie weaved her way around the tables, past the plant crates and onto the footpath, pounding the concrete, ploughing through a crowd of pedestrians, scattering pigeons. She ran until she reached the smaller street they'd approached from and turned the corner. Someone crashed into her, spun her around. It was Julian, his face blazing with some emotion Cassie couldn't even recognise. He had her by the arms and she realised he was trying to stop her pummelling him. Or more accurately, he was allowing her to punch out at him, but slowing the force of the blows to his stomach. She stopped. What was she doing? A hot flood of shame washed through her. He maintained his grip around her wrists, a wariness stealing across his features, replacing the burning that had made his eyes seem so dark and his brown skin pale.

"Have you finished?" His voice was steady, belying everything she'd just seen on his face.

The threatening sting of tears made her look away, but she could feel his gaze on her, his nearness. She didn't want to hit him anymore. She definitely did not want that.

Ali rounded the corner. Julian let go. Relief was again evident in Ali's eyes. Guilt hit Cassie in the stomach like one of her own punches and she bowed her head. How many more times would she make them worry about her? As the fierce strength washed from her muscles, she resolved that the answer would be never again.

Ali spoke carefully, eyeing Cassie as though she were a wild animal ready to bolt. "I have some good news. I know where we are."

ONCE MORE, they followed Ali along back lanes and up busy streets until they were in the heart of the city. This was definitely Melbourne, Cassie's city. Long silver trams replaced the cars, and the buildings became older and taller, interspersed with gleaming skyscrapers. Cassie thought she too recognised where they were now. Yes, they were near the river and the Arts Centre. Her heart kicked up a beat. What if Mum's work was somewhere close by? She wished she knew where her office was. In all her sixteen years, Cassie had never visited her mother at work. Whenever they'd met up with her in the city, it had always been in the Botanic Gardens, the Museum, the Gallery or the State Library. It seemed to be the library that Ali was leading them up the hill to now.

The State Library was one of Cassie's favourite places in Melbourne, and her most treasured part of it was the domed reading room with its enormous oculus to the sky: a massive octagonal window, surrounded by smaller windows held by struts fanning out across the roof like a white spider web, allowing light in from all directions. As soon as they'd hurried up the long grey steps and entered the library's dignified hush, Cassie took the lead, pulling them into the reading room, her whole being thrumming with its familiarity. She led them to an unoccupied wooden desk lit with frosted green lamps and threw herself into a chair. The others followed suit, sliding into the nearby chairs. Ali seemed just as much at home, her peaceful smile reflecting Cassie's own. Only Julian seemed ill at ease.

"What are we doing here?" he whispered.

"Welcome to my second home," said Ali.

Cassie caressed the polished wood beneath her hands and looked up at Ali's beaming face. "Wish it were *my* second home. How long have you been coming here?"

"For years," she said simply.

Julian frowned. And then a pained, yearning look flickered across his face. Ali placed her hand on his arm.

"All the research I've done will help you too, Julian." She stood up. "I'll be back in a minute."

Cassie's contentment was abruptly broken by Ali's departure. Julian sat stiffly, his gaze directed downwards.

She wasn't sure she could bring herself to meet his eyes anyway.

"I'm sorry I tried to hurt you," she whispered.

His eyes flickered, but he didn't look up. He just opened out his hand as though examining something invisible in his palm.

When he spoke, his voice was quiet. "It's okay. You didn't hurt me."

He raised his eyes to hers, and a little jolt travelled down through her body.

"I wanted to," she said. "I wanted to hurt you."

"Why?" He seemed truly curious.

"Because I miss you." The answer burst from her. "Because I'm angry that you left me and came back a different person."

It was more than she'd meant to say and not all she wanted to say. But it felt true.

He stared at her, and her cheeks flushed under his intense scrutiny.

"I didn't think that would be the reason," he said finally.

He moved his hand so that it hovered over hers for a moment, before lowering it, touching her slowly as though afraid she might pull away.

"Why?" The library faded around her, her vision becoming a circle filled only with Julian. "Why else would I possibly want to hurt you?"

She watched his mouth moving, his lips forming words. "Because your kind doesn't tend to like my kind."

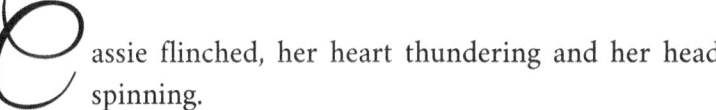assie flinched, her heart thundering and her head spinning.

"What do you mean?"

The hush of the library was like a blanket absorbing all sound. Instead of answering, Julian removed his hand from hers and traced a circle with his finger in the dust that had gathered near the partition between the desks. In the centre, he drew a flower with five petals.

He looked up from the drawing and fixed her with a hard stare. "You protected us. Yet you say you don't understand."

Cassie shook her head and exhaled a short, hard breath of frustration. "Julian, please."

He examined her face quizzically now. "You really don't know?"

Cassie's stomach squirmed, and her face reddened. Again. A child who knew nothing.

Before Julian could explain further, Ali appeared, carrying a thick, old-looking book covered in grass green cloth, embossed on the spine with faint, gold lettering. She placed it onto the table in front of them, disturbing a puff of dust that rose and landed in a thin film over Julian's drawing.

"This is what I was looking for," she said, triumphant, opening the book to the middle and flicking through a few pages. "Here..." She ran her finger down several paragraphs, until she stopped, stabbing halfway down the page. "This is it."

She shifted the book so that Cassie and Julian could read it.

> 'The night it is gude Halloween,
> The fairy folk do ride,
> And they that wad their true-love win,
> At Miles Cross they maun bide.'

"It's part of *Tam Lin*," said Ali, "A Scottish folk ballad thought to originate from some time in the early 1500s. This version is from 1791, one of those collated by Francis Child."

They looked at her blankly.

She sighed. "The old stories encode a lot of lore. What I want to do has been done before. Halloween, see?"

Julian frowned. "But that's over six months away."

"Not for us." She turned a few pages. "Look at this next version."

> 'The morn at even is Halloween;
> Our fairy court will ride,
> Throw England and Scotland both,
> Throw al the world wide:'

She paused, as though waiting for them to catch up. "*Through all the world wide*. Which means us in the southern hemisphere as well."

"But their Halloween's in autumn. And our seasons don't exactly match theirs—if you go by the Kulin seasons, we have seven of them!" said Julian.

"True. But it's not so much about seasons. Halloween, or its older name, Samhain, traditionally represents an astronomical Cross-Quarter date—a mid-point between solstice and equinox. The earth has shifted slightly in relation to the stars since it was first designated. In the northern hemisphere, the Samhain Cross-Quarter now occurs around the 7th of November and the equivalent southern hemisphere Cross-Quarter date this year is the 5th of May."

"That's only a few days away!" said Cassie.

"Exactly. And for whatever reason, stories across the globe suggest that this is the time the veil between the worlds is thinnest. The Dark Cross-Quarter. Our last chance to harvest what we planted, find what we have lost."

Cassie shivered. "Find Tomas, you mean?"

Ali glanced at her and took in Julian's startled expression. "Yes. And also, maybe..." she trailed off, looking at him. He took a deep breath, then nodded and lowered his head. Ali's whisper carried easily in the stillness: "Julian's mother."

Cassie gasped. A man at a nearby desk looked up from his work at them. Cassie waited for him to return to his reading, her whole body shaking. "Violeta?" Her name caught in Cassie's throat.

Julian met her eyes, and she could see all the grief etched there as though he had lost her only yesterday. And she saw something else too: a sense of determination in the set of his chin, as if he were challenging her to disagree with him.

"But I don't understand. You can't bring her back from the..." She couldn't continue. She couldn't say the word.

He shook his head. "She's not dead."

Was this how he had dealt with her loss all these years?

Why he hadn't wanted to talk about her? Because that way he could believe that she was still present somehow, still alive somewhere.

She opened her mouth, closed it again. And how had Ali become involved? Why was she encouraging his delusion? She turned to Ali, trying to read her motivation. They didn't really know her, after all. What if she were leading them astray, pulling the two of them into something darker—a cult, a coven, or whatever was going on here? Suddenly, the hush of the library seemed to press in on her, its domed walls pushing in from all sides like a cocoon. She would not let herself be torn apart and remade into whatever creature this young woman wanted them to become. It was time to leave. To simply head to the station, catch a train and find her way home. She could do it. She knew where she was now. She stood up and pushed her chair back. A flicker of confusion crossed Ali's features.

But it was Julian who spoke to her in a loud whisper, "What are you doing, Cassie?"

"I'm going home."

"But I need you."

She turned around, fighting the pulling feeling in her stomach, and her words came out as a snarl, "I thought you said your kind doesn't like my kind. Whatever that means."

Out of the corner of her eye, she noticed Ali's eyebrows dart upwards.

Julian let out what sounded like a disparaging laugh. "You've got it backwards."

Cassie felt heat flashing across her cheeks and a roaring like the sea in her ears.

"Cassie, will you at least let us walk with you?" said Ali, standing up quickly.

"No."

She strode to the door that led out of the reading room. Ali caught up. "Please. I owe that to your parents."

"I'm not a child," she hissed, striding through the doorway.

Julian appeared beside her. Cassie turned in exasperation, then looked from his face to Ali's and back to his again. She had promised herself she wouldn't walk off on them again. Where was that resolve now? She slowed down.

"I know you're not," Ali was saying. "Let's go somewhere we can talk more freely then. Can we do that?"

Cassie breathed in and out, trying to steady herself. "Fine. But you need to tell me everything. Or I'm going home."

Ali led them up a staircase to a quiet nook by a window with a couple of soft couches. Ali sat on one and Cassie flung herself onto the other, while Julian leaned against the window frame, staring out at the sky with an unreadable expression.

Ali bent forward and touched Cassie's knee. "It's understandable that you're in a bit of shock. What you've experienced over the last two days would be enough to cause most people to book themselves into a psych ward."

She paused, and Cassie felt that breathing might stop Ali from talking. She took a quick gulp of air and tried to look calm as Ali scrutinised her. Whatever Ali saw on her face seemed enough to encourage her to continue.

"But you're mentally tougher than that. I knew it as soon as I began helping you with your schoolwork. You grasp things quickly and you're eager to see through puzzles to get to the truth of things."

A quiet laugh came from Julian's direction. He had his hands in his pockets and was watching a pigeon preening itself on a nearby roof gutter. Cassie glanced at him, frowning, then turned pointedly back to Ali. "Go on."

"I have been searching for my friend Tomas for almost six years now. Learning all I could about how I might gain access again to the world between worlds. I've had help; one of my dearest friends, Nellie, has also been keeping her ear to the ground for me. A few months ago, she heard tell of a family with an ancient duty, a role that they and their descendants have been carrying out for generations. One member of this family moved to Curwood about 20 years ago and began a family of their own."

Julian turned from the window. Cassie could feel his gaze on her now.

"I was curious," Ali continued. "I thought I might learn something from this family. I knew where they lived, and at first I was simply going to call by, find out what I could and leave. But honestly, I was a little"—she glanced at Julian, who was listening intently now—"wary. I wasn't sure the direct approach would be entirely safe for me. I felt I had to find out a little more about them first. I discovered they had a young person at home who didn't go to school, so I left a letter in their mailbox with my number and website, offering my tutoring services."

"*My* family?" Cassie could feel her brain struggling to catch up, jumping from fact to fact as though each one was a fast-melting iceberg in a boiling sea.

Ali nodded. "Now I see that your parents would have arrived in Curwood around the time that your father," she turned to Julian, "brought home his new bride. Would that be right?"

Julian narrowed his eyes. "Yes, I'd say so."

She turned back to Cassie. "Haven't you wondered how you could do it?"

"Do it? You mean that thing with the flowers?"

Ali smiled. "Yes, that thing with the flowers. Did your mother teach you?"

Cassie frowned, trying to remember. "No," she said slowly after a time, "I don't think so. Dad has taught me more about plants than Mum. He tends Mum's herb garden for her. She just tells him what she wants in there."

"Interesting."

Cassie felt her face grow hot. "I didn't know what I was doing, you know. It wasn't, like, a conscious thing."

"Did it feel as though it was just flowing through you?"

She turned to Julian, surprised that he'd spoken. He had uncrossed his arms and was eyeing her with more curiosity than anything else now.

"Yes, that's exactly what it felt like."

"I get that," he said quietly.

"You do?" Cassie breathed out and leaned against the back of the couch.

"Yeah. When I play piano. Sometimes tunes just arrive and my fingers play them. But they're like visitors. If I don't catch them, they're gone, off out the window like they have somewhere else to be."

Cassie nodded, hearing a medley of Julian's haunting melodies run through her mind, the ones he had captured, she supposed. "That's pretty much what it was like."

Ali nodded slowly. "Well, that makes a kind of sense. I didn't know that could happen...but then again, I didn't really believe your kind existed until recently."

"My kind? You two keep saying that." Clouds were knitting together outside the window behind Julian, and Cassie shivered, remembering the tug of the smothering fog. "Will you tell me what *my kind* is?"

Ali wet her lips with her tongue and turned to look

behind her, checking, Cassie supposed, that their alcove was empty. Then she leaned in.

"You, Cassie, are descended from a very long line of Spiritweavers. Some people would call them witches, but that's just one of their names. These wild witches or solitary green witches are those whose magical skills are wrought from the land, from an understanding of, and communion with, plants and wild creatures and elements of the earth. Others might call them shamans. It just depends on where you are in the world, really. As far as I can work out, the Spiritweaver who was your descendant came out here on one of the early ships from Europe. Prior to his or her arrival, the work was, and in many places still is, carried out by local Spiritweavers. Nellie tells me that as a child, she met one of these local Weavers, and that this particular Spiritweaver was powerful enough to rescue her own lover from the world between worlds. They had a son. Whom I met." Her voice grew quiet, wistful. "His name was Jack." She trailed off and turned to the gathering clouds.

"What happened to him?" asked Cassie quietly.

Ali's eyes flickered, and she smiled. "I believe he is still carrying on his mother's task. There are Spiritweavers in both our world and the other. Working from both sides, if you will."

It was hard to find words after that. Cassie supposed that all that Ali was saying must be true, because she could feel no protest anywhere within her at this revelation. It was as if she'd already known it. A vision of her mother's locked book, currently hidden under Cassie's bed, floated in her mind's eye, and she felt again the knowing that it was a thing of moonlight, of the night. A fierce longing for her mother overcame her. The longing was a visceral thing, squeezing her heart. She buckled over, brought her hand to the ache in her chest. Lyra would have known what to do, could have explained all this to her. She rocked a little, the way Mum had rocked her in her arms as a baby. This was not how it was meant to go. She saw it in a flash: there would have been a rite amongst the trees, a solemn ceremony under the gaze of the bright, full moon. And she would have been gifted with the correct words, the right knowing.

Centuries of faces of young women, their hair wreathed in flowers, flashed like cards being flipped before her eyes. All those who had gone before her. That was how she should have found out. With her mother's hand in hers, linked to all the grandmothers before them, connected back to the ancient way, the first Spiritweaver in her family. The first wise daughter.

"It was a woman," whispered Cassie.

"What?" said Ali, blinking.

"It has always been the women in my family."

Julian's stare grew hard.

"Don't ask me how I know," said Cassie quietly, turning to stare outside at the grey sky, "I just do."

hey felt the first fine sprinklings of rain as they made their way out onto the street. Ali had an idea where they could stay the night and was now striding ahead of them towards what had to be one of the last phone boxes in the city. Cassie watched her, hoping it'd take Ali's bankcard.

The rain became heavier, and the wind picked up, funnelling the icy cold change through the skyscraper-lined streets. It was only when Julian drew her under the shelter of a tram stop that she realised she was shivering. He didn't seem cold in his t-shirt, his dark gold skin still smooth, not all goose-pimpled like hers. She pulled her hair out of its messy braid to keep her shoulders warmer.

"You're freezing." He was looking down at her, his eyes very dark.

She nodded, and he spun her on the spot and wrapped his arms around her in one liquid movement, shielding her back from the wind.

"Better?"

"Yes."

His warmth radiated all through her until there was nothing within her that was not alive with sparking heat. She could smell his scent now too: salt and an earthy spice.

Ali burst, breathless, into the shelter. "I've booked us a hotel," she said, shaking the water out of her hair. She glanced at them and tilted her head to the side, her lips twitching into a smile. "Three rooms."

Julian released Cassie and stepped back. "Lead on."

Cassie nodded, shivering again as the cold air stole back up her spine.

By the time they reached the glowing hotel lobby, Cassie was starving. While Ali checked them in, Julian bent low, examining something in a glass case beside a door that, from the sounds of scraping cutlery, music and the hum of conversation, led to the in-house restaurant. Her stomach gurgled.

She wandered over to have a peek. In the far corner of the restaurant, she could see one table still free.

"Phew, I'm starving."

Julian glanced up at her. "Cas, look at this."

She joined him in his squat beside the glass case. He was pointing at a photograph, by the looks of it a very old one, in sepia, from a time before the city of Melbourne had paved roads. Women in Victorian dresses and men in suits and top hats crossed the street or walked alongside horse-drawn carts. It was fascinating, and eerie too, to think that none of these people were alive anymore. All their comings and goings, all the things they thought were important, everything they cared about on that sunny day, meant nothing to anyone now.

"It's kind of beautiful," she said, "and sad."

He frowned and followed her gaze. "Do you mean the photograph?"

"Yes, isn't that what—"

"No, behind it."

She moved closer to him. At his angle, she could see what he'd been staring at. It was a necklace, draped over a black velvet mannequin neck, that looked as though it might once have belonged to one of those long-dead Victorian ladies. The chain was an aged gold metal, and hanging from it, set within an intricate looping border of beaten gold, was a bright stone shaped into a five-pointed flower. Its colour was exactly the light purplish blue of fresh borage flowers.

"Starflower," she whispered.

Julian's eyes widened as he looked at her. "What?"

"That's the other name for borage. But why is it here?"

He shook his head. "I thought you might know."

"I don't." She touched the hollow above her collarbone. "It's so beautiful." The light in the stone seemed to dance under the lobby's many hanging bulbs. "Its colour. I've always wondered..." She tailed off, staring into its glowing depths as though she could dissolve into it.

"Imperial Purple." Julian's answer surprised her out of her reverie.

"Imperial?"

"I remember it from my pencil set at home. I've used it before. Drawing your garden."

Cassie raised her eyebrows. She looked down at his long, fine, strong fingers, resting lightly over his knees now as he crouched. She had watched those fingers move so deftly across the keys of the piano, but she'd never seen him draw. Of course, Mr Walcott had made sure his son was schooled in all the Arts. But she hadn't known he liked to draw. And that felt strange.

"You've drawn...my garden?"

His cheeks darkened. "Yes. Many times."

She stared at him. "I didn't know. That you could draw, I mean. What about *your* garden?"

"I draw that too. And other things." He met her eyes, and she felt heat rise in her face. "But your garden is perfect."

She opened her mouth, releasing her breath in a rush. "You live in a manor! With all that beautiful, landscaped space..."

He shook his head. "No, you don't understand. Your garden, there you can be free."

"All booked in!" Ali called to them from the counter. "Ready to go?"

Cassie got hastily to her feet. "Yes."

Julian sprang up next to her, his movements fluid and precise. She'd never thought of him as graceful before; in fact, she'd always prided herself on being the one who could dance longer, run faster, climb higher. He'd been the one to watch her with his quiet, reflective eyes. The one who, more than she ever had, lived in his mind, his music, his books. But as she watched him walk after Ali, she could see now that he fully inhabited his own body; more than that, in the time he'd been away, he had found a kind of mastery, a flow between body, heart and mind. Of all the things that had changed, had turned her world inside out lately, this one at least, made her happy.

Her room was between Ali's and Julian's. She slid in the key card and pushed open the door.

Ali leaned out from her own room. "Dinner downstairs in half an hour?"

Cassie's stomach growled. "Twenty minutes?"

Ali grinned, her eyes glimmering in the dim light of the corridor. "Sure."

The room had the comforting smell of washed bed linen and looked neat and comfortable, with heavy dark curtains pulled across the window. She tugged open the curtains and golden sunset light flooded the room. Her view was onto a stone balcony that looked out over rooftops and the red brick wall of a building on the street below.

A pang that was not hunger struck her now. Being in a hotel room had always meant Mum was nearby—an association formed since babyhood from the many times they'd stayed in the city with her on her extended work trips. On the times when Dad had stayed behind at home, she would spend her days in a hotel room doing schoolwork, or reading or crafting, and Lyra would meet up with her in the afternoons for a trip to the Museum or a play at the Arts Centre or at the very least an Italian dinner in Lygon Street. She hugged her arms around herself.

There was an old black telephone by her bed. She picked up the receiver. She knew how to dial out from a hotel. Had done it many times before. Her fingers dialled her dad's number. What would she say when he picked up? Would she ask him where he'd been? Why he had left her alone? A hot, quick anger rose in her. Then, as the dial tone blinked on and on with no answer until it rang out, a cold stab of fear froze the heat that had been rushing through her veins until she ached with it. The knowledge that she hadn't wanted to see sat like a dark thing in the corner of her mind, and she could almost hear its soft, feral laugh. *He's gone. Your Daddy's gone.*

She slammed the phone back on its hook and stalked into the bathroom, stripped off her clothes and ran the shower on full blast. It took a lot of hot water and rich scented hotel shampoo to thaw the ice inside her.

She opened her door at the same time Julian was exiting his room. He had taken a shower too, although while she'd found the hairdryer stashed in the second drawer in the bathroom, his towel-dried hair was dampening the shoulders of his t-shirt. His freshly washed face looked younger. It reminded her of swimming together at the swimming hole, the days fighting for space on the one flat rock that was always deliciously hot on their skin, and the drawings they made on its black surface with drips from their hair or the damp imprints of their palms.

He gave her a small smile before taking the stairs in front of her and it produced a little ache beneath her ribcage, because his smile was such a rare thing, like glimpsing a species of butterfly that had once been common but had now almost faded from the world. She watched his back, his economical movements, as he took the stairs two-by-two.

"Hungry?"

Cassie started. Ali was quietly descending the stairs behind her.

"Yes." She waited for Ali on her step. "I'm sorry I don't have any money with me to pay for anything."

Ali's laughter echoed in the stairwell. "I think you mean, I'm sorry you dragged me from my home, whisked me through a magic portal and left me to fight a ravenous fog monster on my own. No, Cassie my dear, the apologies are all mine."

By the time they'd settled themselves at the table in the far corner of the restaurant, the crowd of diners had thinned a little. The ceiling was hung with industrial pendant lights with bulbs the colour of orange flame. In contrast, the walls were an aged white, decorated all around with vertical raised plaster wall panels covered with elaborate, curling designs. Julian leaned back against one of these panels as he read the menu, the leaf-patterned boughs winding behind his head like a pale green crown.

After the waiter—a tall, young man with a soft white face and large hands—had taken their orders, Ali leaned forward.

"I've invited a friend of mine to join us. She should be here any minute. Her name's Rebecca."

Julian raised his eyebrows briefly and took a drink of his water. "Okay."

Ali turned to Cassie. "I want to let her know what we've found so far. She's his sister—Tomas's."

Cassie felt her mouth open in astonishment, but before she could form words into any sensible order, Ali had pushed back her chair and was striding over to embrace the young woman who'd just walked into the restaurant. As Ali ushered her lost friend's sister towards their table, Cassie eyed Rebecca curiously. She had long, dark brown hair, a pale, oval face and was wearing a red vintage dress sprinkled with small white dots, teal leggings and short burgundy boots.

As she sat at their table, she gave them a small wave. Her fingers were long and artistic, but her nails were short and unvarnished. Cassie supposed she was only a year or two older than herself and Julian, but it was hard to tell, as she had the self-possessed air of someone much older.

"Hi."

Julian nodded and Cassie smiled as Ali sat down next to her.

"Rebecca, meet Cassie and Julian," said Ali, her eyes shimmering with the reflection of the fire-coloured lights as she waved toward each of them. She looked like a wild queen holding court in a fairy grotto. "Rebecca's at university here in the city, aren't you?"

Rebecca nodded.

"What are you studying?" asked Julian. His face, though

politely curious, held a subtle wariness, a tension around his jaw that Cassie, who'd known him so long, could read.

"Maths/Physics major. At Melbourne Uni."

This surprised Cassie. She'd presumed, from the way she was dressed, the feel of her presence, that she was an Arts student. "Wow. That's cool."

Rebecca smiled at her, and it reminded her of Julian, brought the same familiar ache to her chest. What Cassie had taken for self-possession, she now realised, was something else; grief for her brother was the easy guess. Like Julian, Rebecca had removed herself slightly from the world. Snow White, unreachable in her glass case.

"Rebecca wants to specialise in Cosmology, don't you?" Ali turned to her friend.

Rebecca nodded. "Yes, I'm hoping to do my Masters next year. I'm interested in the structure of the Universe; how it's shaped, what it's made of, the mathematics of dimensions, time...all that."

The language of the Universe, Cassie. "Your way of finding your brother." Cassie felt her cheeks go red as she realised she'd spoken these last words aloud and that Rebecca was staring at her. "I'm so sorry—"

Rebecca raised her palm. "No. Don't apologise. You're correct." She looked at Ali. "We've both been doing what we can in our own ways."

Julian leaned forward, his chin on steepled fingers. He looked tired, she thought, with dark shadows beneath his eyes. "Any insights then?"

Rebecca turned to Julian with a thoughtful gaze. "None yet. Not really. Nothing you couldn't get from any half-baked science fiction novel. I believe the 'world between worlds', as Ali calls it, is a localised pocket of the Universe with different physical Laws. What I find more fascinating is that its time axis is out of sync with ours. For us, it seems to exist only every seven years. I have no idea how that can be possible."

"What about the pieces of that world that Weavers can travel through? Alisa calls them 'bubbles'," said Julian with a nod to Ali.

Rebecca breathed out slowly and shook her head. "I don't know. Ali tells me you experienced one."

"It was as real as this restaurant," whispered Cassie.

Rebecca nodded slowly. "I remember."

Cassie blinked in surprise. Julian leaned further forward, his hands clasped together on the table now.

"Rebecca was trapped in one of those pockets with her brother," said Ali.

"Until you rescued me." Rebecca smiled wanly, her hand reaching out to rest on Ali's arm.

But not Tomas, seemed to be the loud, unspoken words between them. Ali lowered her gaze to the polished wood of the table.

Rebecca picked up the menu in front of her. "I should order something."

"Then why can't we get in the way you did, Ali?" asked Cassie.

"I've tried to, many times since. But the way is closed. I don't know if it will be forever, or whether it only opens every seven years. I believe I visited the world between worlds then. Maybe I came out via a bubble. I don't know exactly."

Cassie and Julian ate their steaming pasta in silence after that as Ali talked softly, filling Rebecca in on their journey to the city. By the time Rebecca's food arrived, Cassie found herself fighting against a crushing wave of tiredness.

"Ali," she said during a lull in their dialogue, "I'm going upstairs. I need to sleep."

"Of course. Rest. I'll order breakfast for us. See you in the morning."

As Cassie rose, Julian pushed out his chair. "I'll head up too." He turned politely to Rebecca. "Good to meet you."

Rebecca's face was wistful as they bid her goodnight.

"Take care, both of you," she said. "We only know what our senses grant us access to. Microscopes and telescopes can take us further. But sometimes even they cannot see far enough. Good luck."

13

---

*J*ulian watched Cassie ascend the stairs. Light gleamed on her long, loose curls. He wanted to touch them, to slide them between his fingers the way he had as a kid and feel them spring back in his hands.

The girl in front of him had lengthened like a willow in the time he'd been away; all her childish curves turned to strength. She had the same maddening determination—gumption, his father had called it, in one of the very few conversations they'd ever had about Cassie. He knew Cassie thought John Walcott despised her, but Julian knew this wasn't true. His father had always had a strange respect for her, one that bordered on fear of her influence over his son. And how she *had* influenced him, in so many ways. At first, he'd found it frustrating, shameful almost, that she could beat him in all things physical. But the awe he felt watching her scamper up a tree, her fearlessness when she ran, or leapt between rocks in the river, all this, had inspired him to try harder, be braver, to go where he'd never have ventured without her. She'd always been his wild flame, whipping up a burning desire in him to do more, be more, to be strong, and free.

The burning was still there. But it was different now. In the way she was different. The way he was different. During his time away from her, he had trained hard, taken up everything he could at the new school: fencing, archery, taekwondo, and music too; his beloved piano—embracing every chance he could to get out of his head. And it felt good, kept the fire alive in him while he was not with her.

Now that he was near her, he found the fire hard to contain within the boundaries of his own body. And the new knowledge he had about her made it worse somehow, tinging the burning with fear and doubt. Yes, she remained his childhood friend, but she was also something else. Something dangerous. And he wanted her in a way he never had. The demons of fear and desire were treating him like roadkill to be fought over, pushing and pulling, eating him up.

Yet there was the trust, the beautiful trust he'd always had in the Cassie he knew; the sweet, wild girl she was. Could he still hold onto that?

They were at their doors. She'd already slid in her key card with quick fingers.

"Cassie."

She turned to him, her eyes widening a little. Her collarbone was smooth and light gold. He wondered what it would feel like beneath his fingers. He raised his hand, lowered it again.

"Goodnight."

A furrow flickered between her eyebrows. She searched his face, her lips parted. Heat rose to his cheeks.

"Goodnight, Julian."

And then she was gone, her door closing after her with a quiet click.

~

CASSIE LAY in her bed with its smell of soap and metal. She'd expected fall asleep easily, but the heaviness in her, the spell of the warm restaurant and the food in her belly had worn off and now she was alert and restless. No amount of shifting from side to side, staring up at the ceiling or squeezing her eyes shut helped. She sat up and stared through the gauzy inner curtains at the city lights that blurred and washed together like an impressionist painting.

It was too hot in here. She pulled on her clothes, crossed to the glass door and slid it open. Stepping out into the frigid air was a relief. The wind had died down, and the sky was black, studded to the horizon with red and gold city lights like electric stars.

A bass line floated up from somewhere below, thumping in her chest like an extra heartbeat. Traffic horns and rolling trams layered in to form a musical piece that was nothing like the night melodies of crickets and owls and the whispers of leaf on leaf at home.

She pulled in a deep, icy breath and turned to go inside, but a movement caught her eye.

"Julian?"

She hadn't noticed him across the low wall that separated their balconies, standing as still as the stone itself, staring out over the city.

He turned to her, only half his face lit by the light from his room. "Can't sleep?"

"No."

"Me neither."

She hugged her arms around herself. "Can I come over?"

He said nothing for a moment, then swallowed and gave her a nod. "Yes. Of course."

It took only a moment before she was out in the corridor, standing in front of Julian's door. He opened it silently and let her in. He had bare feet too and was still in his jeans and t-shirt. His room was much like hers, only with the bed on the opposite wall.

"Hot drink?" he asked, filling the kettle.

She nodded her thanks, walked across to his window, and stared into the night. "I can't help wondering if Mum's out there somewhere."

He came up behind her with a blanket and wrapped it around her shoulders.

She spun around to him. "Neither of them are answering their phones. I just don't understand where Dad could be, what's happened to him. He never doesn't answer."

Julian pulled a chair out for her, but she sat on his bed, and he took the chair instead.

"I don't understand it either." He leaned forward, elbows on knees. "But I think we're all in danger, your parents included. I just hope they managed to get away before he found them."

Cassie shook her head. "The Weaver? What would he want with my parents?"

The kettle boiled and clicked off. Julian got to his feet, searched the cupboards, and finally placed two white mugs carefully on the bench in front of him.

"I went to find the Weaver, about a week before all this happened."

"To *find* him?"

He sorted through the bowl of sachets and teabags, nodding slowly.

"He had that cockatoo of his spying on us, both your family and mine, for who knows how long before I worked it out. I followed the bird back to his place, and that's when I realised." His gaze flicked to hers.

"Realised what?"

"That I'd seen him before. A long time ago. When my mother first went missing."

"Went missing? You mean..."

Julian shook his head. "She didn't die, Cassie. She disappeared."

"But I, you...we were at the memorial service...your dad—"

"My father lied."

"But why would he do that?" she countered gently.

He shoved the sachets back into their bowl, frustration in every taut line of his body.

"My father's a proud man. You, of all people, know that."

Cassie met his gaze. "Yes. I do."

"Well there were certain...things...about my mother that she hid from him, things she knew he'd never accept."

He sighed abruptly and shook his head, then he moved to the bed and sat down next to her, taking hold of her hand. The unexpected touch sent a bolt through her. His gaze was entreating, begging her to believe him, his eyes feverishly bright. She opened her mouth then closed it again, forcing herself to be quiet enough to hear him through.

"The night the Weaver came, she tried to defend herself. And my father saw, for the first time, what my mother was like when she was angry, provoked. It frightened and disgusted him. He let the Weaver take her. And then..." He released her hand, his jaw tightening. "He pretended she was dead."

Cassie said nothing. There was so much she wanted to

say. To ask. But she found she couldn't. Julian's face was so full of anger and anguish, a pain as present now as on the day his mother had vanished from their lives.

She touched a hand to his cheek. He bowed his head, his lips brushing her thumb, the pulse at his throat fluttering against her fingers. Then he grasped her hand and pressed her palm against his chest. She could feel heat through his shirt and the deep beat of his heart. Blood roared in her ears, and she didn't want to move or breathe. The lamplight picked out the plane of his jaw, the smooth line of his mouth, so near hers. She leaned into him.

But in an instant he was gone, leaping from the bed in a movement so fast and fluid she barely had time to register it; and now he stood on the other side of the room, his face pale.

"You should go."

She flinched. "Julian?"

"Please go."

She lifted her chin, her heart tightening sharply in her chest, and got to her feet. The blanket fell from her shoulders.

He turned to the window.

Blinking to keep her childish tears from betraying her, she strode out of the room and shoved the door closed behind her. But instead of the satisfying slamming noise she had expected, the soft-hinged door closed achingly slowly between them. She glared through the narrowing gap.

He was standing dead still, staring after her, his eyes alight from within with an impossible, unearthly flicker of orange fire.

14

*C*assie stayed in her room for breakfast: cold toast, orange juice, and lukewarm coffee. She ate in a daze, watching the city sky lighten, feeling the thrum of human activity building in the street below. Ali had said nothing of their plans for today, how long they could stay here or when it might be safe for Cassie to return home. She tried calling her mum again, then her dad, twice, with no more success than the night before.

She'd been expecting a knock on her door, but still jumped at the sound when it came. She opened it wide but stepped back in surprise when she saw that it was not Ali, but a small girl with bright green eyes and dark red hair that fell about her in waves like shining ribbons. She wore a forest green dress with long tan boots and she was standing with her hands behind her back.

"Hello, can I come in?"

Cassie took another step backwards. "Ah, I think you might have the wrong room."

"You *are* Cassie, aren't you?" asked the girl, pushing in past her.

Cassie frowned and closed the door. "Yes. But who are you?"

The girl turned to face her and brought her arms out from behind her back. In her hands, pulsing with light, lay the starflower necklace she and Julian had seen in the cabinet.

"Grandma says to give you this. She says it's been waiting for you. But not to tell my mum."

"Your mum? Um, sorry, who—"

"I'm Selene and my mum owns this hotel."

"Look, Selene, thank you, but I can't just take this. It belongs to someone else. And I don't want to make your mother upset."

Selene shook her head. "No. Grandma says it belongs to you."

Cassie's eyebrows knitted in confusion. "I...I can't. I'm sorry."

"Please," said Selene, reaching for Cassie's hand and pressing the necklace into her palm. "Don't worry about Mum. She's not a Weaver, she doesn't understand."

Cassie stared at the little girl. "And are you...a Weaver?"

Selene laughed. "No silly. That's Grandma. She's been waiting for you to arrive."

"Well. Ah, where is she? Your Grandma?"

"Why?"

"Well, if I'm going to take this necklace, I'd like to thank her."

"I'm sorry. You can't. Grandma's not alive anymore."

Cassie stared at Selene, and it felt like falling.

"I have to go now." She made her way back towards the door. "Goodbye, Cassie."

And before Cassie could say a thing, the girl had whipped out of the room.

Cassie raced to the door. "Wait!"

But when she looked down the corridor, she couldn't see her. Instead, she saw a streak of red and the bushy tail of what was most distinctly a fox disappearing down the stairs. By the time she'd grabbed her key card and raced down into the foyer, there was no sign of either fox or girl.

"Selene!"

Cassie ran out of the hotel and down the front steps.

"Selene! Come back!"

The footpath moved swiftly beneath her feet and the air took on a sharp, crystalline quality, making all the colours around her bright and clear. Everything was still, even though she was running. Cars seemed to drive with infinite slowness and she found she could easily wend her way around them to cross the road to the other side, following the sparkling thread of fox.

She found herself heading down a set of bluestone steps to the river and spotted the fox by a tree in rich autumn leaf.

"Selene!"

The fox turned towards her and began to spin on the spot in slow motion—a graceful whirl that lifted the orange leaves carpeting the steps into a spinning dance, until a young girl stood before Cassie, her eyes wide and her mouth forming a perfect circle of surprise.

Cassie came to a halt, her head lashing back as though she'd braked hard in a car. She gasped and dropped her hands to her knees, her lungs working like bellows to bring in enough air. When she looked up, she saw that the fox-girl was watching her, her face alight.

"Grandma was right. Of course."

"Please," she gasped, still fighting for breath, "Please don't go. I need to know more."

Selene stepped lightly from the steps to a patch of grass under the oak and sat down cross-legged

"You're a good tracker, Earthweaver."

Cassie joined her, glad of the cool lawn beneath them.

"Earthweaver?"

Selene eyed her, her head tilted to one side. Then she sighed and reached out her small hand to touch the necklace still clutched in Cassie's hand.

"Put it on."

Cassie obeyed her, clipping the necklace behind her neck. It felt heavy and cold.

Selene smiled. "Now close your eyes. Feel into it. See without your eyes."

Cassie closed her eyes, then flashed them back open. "You won't go?"

Selene shook her head. "Trust me."

Cassie wanted to say something about trusting a fox, but then she would have had to say aloud what still seemed absurd and impossible: that this girl and the fox were one. Instead, she closed her eyes again.

"Can you feel it?"

"What am I supposed to be feeling?"

"Shh, listen without your ears."

Cassie breathed in and out, feeling the weight of the necklace just below her collarbone. It was less cold now, as though it had absorbed some of the heat from her skin. It also felt lighter. It was pleasant, tingling at first and then throbbing like a subtle heartbeat. She had the sensation of something, some energy spinning around her, spreading a warm, vital power through her body. It was gold and sparkling in her mind's eye, filling her veins, spreading from her core out through the muscles of her arms and legs to the very tips of her fingers and toes. She snapped open her eyes and looked down. The starflower jewel was glowing bright blue, like captured lightning.

Selene was beaming at her.

Cassie met her eyes, her mouth open in awe at the ecstatic feeling of power rippling through her body. "What do I do with all this?"

"The necklace is a protection and a prism, designed by early Earthweavers to give you the power to allow this magic of yours to manifest and to channel it as you desire. You're going to need practice, of course, but you get to choose what you do with your power. Mostly, you folk have spent generations using it to keep people like me in check." She grinned. "But don't worry. I'm no threat. And I loved my grandma—who was an Earthweaver like you—more than any of my kind could imagine."

Cassie picked out one of the many questions swirling within her. "Earthweaver? Are they different to Spiritweavers?"

Selene smiled. "An Earthweaver is a type of Spiritweaver —one who works in alignment with the natural world, whose source of power is connection, harmony and the freedom of all living things. Cassie, remember this: you're weaker here in the city. Better to be where there is less iron and tar."

"Okay..." Cassie said slowly, touching her palm to the cool grass. "And...are there other kinds of Spiritweavers?"

Selene crossed her arms and nodded gravely. "Darkweavers. Their source of power is discord and enmity, pain and fear—the friction generated by disharmony."

The incongruity of these words emanating from the

mouth of one who appeared so young struck Cassie before their meaning sank in.

"Selene, have you seen one of these...Darkweavers before?"

The fox-girl's eyes went cold. "Yes. One. He killed Grandma."

Cassie felt suddenly heavy with fear. The necklace stopped glowing. "Oh. I am so sorry."

Selene squared her face so that Cassie was looking directly into the girl's strange green eyes.

"You have to find him, Cassie. And destroy him."

"I don't think...I mean, I can't—"

The girl was all fire and steel. "You can. And you will."

Selene stood up. Cassie hurried to her feet too, her heart thumping, and the fox-girl gave her a quick, fierce hug.

"I have to go. Grandma can only hold the Gate so long. See you again one day."

Then she sped down the steps and away, and all Cassie could see was an orange-red fox's tail disappearing under the bridge.

CASSIE FOUND her way back to the hotel with difficulty, surprised at how far she'd travelled in such a short time. Luckily, the old building rose several storeys above the surrounding shops and cafes, and after a few wrong turns, she was able to reorient herself. At the bottom of the steps leading up to the entrance, she unclipped the necklace and placed it carefully into the pocket of her jeans.

Julian was pacing the foyer when she arrived. As soon as he saw her, he strode over and caught her by the shoulders, his face a study of relief.

"I thought you'd gone."

His voice was rough with worry. It set her reeling with confusion. After last night, she'd been sure she'd done something wrong, had inexplicably made him hate her.

She had no chance to respond though, as Ali ran into the lobby.

"Cassie! Oh, thank heavens!"

"I only went out for a walk."

"Please, don't do that again. Or at least, tell us first. Julian has picked up his trail, the Weaver's. He's close. We need to be more careful." She led them into the dining room. "Come on."

Cassie followed. They headed to the same table as the night before.

"I'll go get us something hot," said Ali, as Cassie and Julian sat down. "Coffee?"

Cassie nodded. "Thanks."

"Julian?"

"No thanks, don't drink the stuff."

Here was something else she didn't know about him. He'd left for boarding school as a kid; there'd been no coffee drinking together in their past. At least this was one small way in which she had changed. Until this moment, it felt as though he'd done all the changing while she stayed the same.

He gave her a small smile. "I'm sorry about last night."

She flushed. "Oh. Um. That's okay."

He took her hand. The heat in her cheeks deepened.

"No. It wasn't okay. I wasn't myself. I never want you to feel unsafe around me."

"Unsafe?"

She blurted out the word without thinking. She hadn't felt unsafe, only hurt and confused. She wanted to say as much, but he was leaning forward, looking into her eyes, and her breath caught in her throat.

"Yes. Because I...care about you, Cassie."

Her heart rate ticked up. "I care about you too."

She caught her lower lip with her teeth. That had sounded feeble. A sudden longing for the ease they'd once had with one another washed through her.

"Julian—"

He sat back, his attention immediately snapping to Ali, who'd just returned from the counter.

Cassie looked down at the tablecloth and tried to compose her face, to dampen the fire in her cheeks and quiet her heart. The necklace in her pocket dug into her thigh.

Ali pulled out her chair. "Right. Here's the deal. The Weaver's in the city, which means Julian's mother could be somewhere here too. He could be hiding her. We're going to find out where."

"I don't get it, though," said Cassie. "Julian, you told me she was taken years ago. Why do you think she's...what makes you sure she's still alive?"

Julian's face darkened. Ali opened her mouth to speak, but he shook his head.

"Alisa, it's all right." He turned to Cassie. "I've seen my mother more recently. We've been in contact...up until a couple of weeks ago. That's why I started looking for her, why I found Ali, and how I realised that bird of his was spying on us. My mother's still alive."

Cassie swallowed. "All right then. So, how do we know she's in the city, not trapped in that...bubble...we came through?"

"Julian would have felt her presence," said Ali. "Things work differently there. Their spirits would have found each other."

"Do we know what the Weaver wants with her?" asked Cassie.

Ali shook her head. "No. But it's unlikely to be anything good. The best we can hope for is that he's simply acting on inbuilt prejudice and mistrust."

Julian hung his head and rubbed at his temples.

Cassie sighed. "Then where do we start?"

15

*W*hatever Cassie had expected, it had not been this. According to Julian, and she had yet to ask how he knew, the Weaver was in here. They were in front of a modern office tower, a gleaming edifice that cut into the sky, sunlight sparking off silver glass and steel.

"Here?"

Julian raised an eyebrow and tilted his head. "Yep."

"Hardly a den of monsterly despair. I had something a lot more gothic in mind," said Cassie.

Ali laughed, her eyes glinting with the reflected light.

The entrance hall was high-ceilinged, with a long desk, and a bewildering choice of elevator buttons lining a gunmetal grey wall to their right.

Julian strode up to the receptionist, a young-looking woman in a white suit, with blonde hair wound up in a sophisticated chignon. Cassie watched with amusement as he leaned forward to talk to her. After a few moments, he beamed a most un-Julian-like smile at her, revealing a flash of white teeth, and sauntered back to them holding a piece of paper.

They spilled out into the eerily neat topiary and gravel space demarcating the office tower from the street. Julian seated himself on a square of concrete doubling as a cover for a spotlight that probably lit up the building at night. Ali and Cassie perched themselves on neighbouring planter boxes.

"List of the businesses that occupy this office tower and three visitor passes," he said, handing the paper and a pass each to Ali and Cassie.

"Good work," Ali said, smiling. "You've got yourself quite some charm there." She began to scan the list.

Julian smiled and met Cassie's gaze. The sunlight catching his eyes set them glimmering. Perhaps that was all she had seen last night; the glow from his bedside lamp. She smiled and shook her head.

"The dazzling Master Walcott."

THEY WERE in the elevator on the way to checking out the first of the businesses Ali had shortlisted when Cassie felt it. It was a sense of untethering, unmooring. Of floating out into somewhere cold and frightening. She gasped inaudibly as the feeling became stronger. Something was being sucked from her, pulled out from her very blood, exactly the reverse of the flowing-in feeling of golden power she'd felt when she'd put on the necklace.

The necklace—maybe it could counteract this awful sensation. She tried to move her hand to her pocket, but her arms were frozen in place. Ali had her back to them, studying the ascending floor numbers, but she felt Julian tense beside her.

"Are you all right?"

She could barely shake her head before her legs collapsed from under her. He bent swiftly, breaking her fall.

Ali spun around in surprise. "Cassie, what is it?"

"Stop the lift!" Julian's voice sounded strange and wavery in her head.

Ali punched at the buttons. The elevator came to a stop with a soft chime and the doors slid open. Julian hauled her out onto a landing lined with hard grey carpet.

"Cassie!" She could feel his hands on either side of her face. "Cassie, what's happening?"

She forced her eyelids to open and tried to move, but her body was floating in a vast, cold ocean and her limbs were stiff and numb. Her eyes found Julian's.

"My pocket. Necklace. Please."

Julian scrabbled at the pocket of her jeans, pulled out the necklace and drew it around her without hesitation, moving her hair aside gently to do up the clasp behind her neck. As soon as the starflower was against her skin, warmth flooded in, melting the ice in her veins until she could move again.

"You're okay?"

Julian searched her face, his dark hair falling across one cheek. For a moment he seemed completely unguarded—the boy on the bridge again. She could see right into him, and what she saw was fierce and tender. He swallowed and pulled her close.

"What the heck *was* that?"

He directed the question to Ali, who was crouched beside them, her pale, beautiful face etched with worry.

"What did you feel, Cassie?" She placed a cool hand against Cassie's forehead.

"It was like something was draining me. Of everything, all vitality, all life. It was horrible."

Ali lowered her voice to a whisper. "I think the Weaver is nearby."

"Do you think you can stand up?" Julian pulled back to examine her.

Cassie gave a small nod and pushed herself to her feet. Her legs felt weak, but she was strong enough to walk.

"What floor were we passing when it happened? Do you remember, Ali?"

"It was number 11, I think. Or 12. I have them on my list.

"Read them out," said Cassie.

"Number 11 is Drake Industries."

"It's that one. Let's go." Cassie punched the elevator button.

"Cassie, we can't be sure—" Ali began

"We can. I know that's the one."

"But you're not well enough."

"I'm all right now." She fingered the necklace.

"No, we should go back to the hotel," Ali insisted, "find another way."

"She can handle it."

They both stared at Julian. The elevator door opened.

"Yes. I can."

Cassie stepped in and they followed her. She pushed number 11 firmly, and the doors slid shut behind them.

The lift opened out onto a bright atrium whose roof was a wide shaft reaching all the way up through the centre of the building. They stepped out onto the white marble floor, blinking. Glass on all sides but one, soaked the internal space with light.

Cassie had the strangest sensation—a rippling, electric feeling across her skin, as though the place was brimming with power. She looked down at the starflower; it was pulsing with its blue light. How could the air feel so full? Then there was the faintest of tugs, the sense again that something was being sucked from her. She folded her fingers around the starflower and closed her eyes, concentrating on bringing the power back into her, pulling it in instead of allowing it to flow outward. As the flow reversed, the golden, electric feeling intensified, and she felt strong and wild and potent, her body tingling and alive. Alive with stolen power.

Someone laughed. The sound came from the corridor to their left, the only place in shadow. The contrast to the light-filled hallway was so great that they couldn't see who stood there, but the laughter was a man's, unnerving and cold.

"I did not take you for a Darkweaver."

Cassie whirled around.

A trim figure in an expensive-looking smoke-grey suit stepped into the light. With a smooth, angular face, short, gold-blond hair and bright blue eyes, he looked to be in his late 20s or 30s, but Cassie suspected he was whatever age he chose to be.

"Staring? Like what you see?"

Julian stepped forward. The man flicked a finger and Julian doubled over as though he'd been punched in the stomach.

"Stay where you are, beast. I will only talk to the Weaver."

"Julian!" Cassie reached for him, but Ali was already pulling him to his feet, watching the man with a mix of fury and fear.

"I'm okay." The rough catch in Julian's voice said otherwise, but he caught her eye and shook his head minutely in warning.

Cassie turned back to the man.

He beamed at her. "While I had hoped, I could not be sure you'd come. I'm glad you did."

"Who are you?" Cassie demanded.

He raised his eyebrows. "Really, Cassie Drake. Do you honestly think I would gift you with my name?"

"You know mine. Or at least, my mother's."

"True." He executed an elegant half-turn. "How about we leave these lesser beings and you and I have a proper chat in my office."

"Absolutely not," said Cassie.

"No," said Ali, "she stays with us."

He gave Cassie a look of such contrived mournfulness that it was almost comic. "In that case, fair sister, I shall most regretfully have to bid you farewell."

"I am not your sister."

"A turn of phrase, nothing more." He looked her up and down in a way that made her shudder. "Although, it did not take you long to discover the delights of the Darkweaver—a mere twenty seconds, I'd say, which does somewhat confirm that we are kin. Most Weavers would not take my power into themselves so easily."

"It's not your power. You stole it."

He tilted his head to the side, his clear blue eyes meeting hers steadily. "As you steal yours from the Earth. How does that make you any better?"

Cassie opened her mouth, then closed it again.

"Precisely. How quickly you see the truth."

"Cassie?" It was Julian.

She wanted to turn to him, but it was as though an invisible wall separated them and she couldn't take her eyes from the Darkweaver's.

"I'll be all right. Get out of here. Wait for me at the hotel."

"No!" Julian leapt forward to grasp her hand, but at a

gesture from the Darkweaver, he staggered back and fell to the floor, clutching at his chest.

"Stop! Stop it!" Cassie screamed.

The Darkweaver turned an impassive face to her. "As you wish."

He flicked a finger again and Julian rolled onto his back, gasping for breath. Ali, who was by his side gripping his hand, now cried out and doubled over in pain.

"Enough! I'll come with you if you promise you'll stop hurting them!"

The Darkweaver looked amused. "I assure you, I am much more interested in you."

Julian struggled to his feet. The Darkweaver took Cassie's hand in his cool one and pulled her away down the corridor. She twisted in his grip to look back. Ali was upright now, with Julian beside her, his hands clenched by his sides. Their eyes met for only a moment before the Weaver jerked her around, but it was long enough to see the flash of fear in his eyes.

As soon as Cassie disappeared from view down the dark corridor, two men materialised either side of Julian and Alisa. One of them, with a slight build and a pinched, hawkish look, grasped Alisa around her shoulders. She flinched, her lips pressing together tightly, but said nothing as he swivelled her towards the stairwell. The other, taller and broader with a metal-grey beard, grabbed Julian by the upper arm. Julian recognised him immediately—the spy, the Weaver, the one who had taken his mother from them.

"This way."

Julian tensed the muscles in his arm. "No."

Alisa glanced at him, her eyes fearful.

The broad man's eyebrows lifted and he tightened his grip. "No?"

Julian planted his feet, centring himself, meeting the man's gaze with a lazy blink of his eyes. "No."

"Come on, Thorne," said the second man, pushing Alisa ahead of him

Julian exhaled loudly through his nose. "Thorne has a debt to pay."

A slow smile stole across the man's face. "The whippet remembers."

"Where is she?"

"Are you referring to your bitch of a mother?"

A spike of pain seared through Julian's jaw as his teeth clenched together. He gave his arm a violent shake, ripping himself out of Thorne's grasp and spinning around to face him.

"Her *name* is Violeta."

Thorne spat. "She was an abomination."

Julian eyed him as steadily as he could with every nerve end screaming at him to run at this man and tear him apart.

"She beat you, didn't she? You were no match for her. You were beaten by a woman." He forced himself to laugh.

Thorne's neck coloured, and his steel-bristled face became blotchy. "She was no woman!"

He sprang at Julian.

Julian stepped lightly aside, and Thorne landed heavily behind him.

He spun around, but Thorne launched at him again, springing from the floor with alarming speed. This time Julian let him throw a punch, pulled at his fist, and used Thorne's own momentum to slam him to the ground. Thorne growled and spun out a kick that knocked Julian off his feet, smashing him against the hard marble tiling, sending a shockwave through his spine. Alisa screamed, and the man holding her yelled something. Julian pushed himself off the floor and locked eyes with Thorne.

"*You* are the abomination," he snarled through a red haze of pain.

Thorne shook his head, his mouth curling, and stretched out an arm, palm towards Julian. "If you say so."

Julian's fingers and toes went cold first, then his arms, his legs, his torso. Thorne was sucking the warmth from him, pulling all that was good and alive from his body, replacing it with ice and fear. This must have been what Cassie had felt, this dying feeling. Her face floated in his mind.

"Your mother's dead, you know. I killed her myself." Thorne's voice cut like a vicious blade.

It wasn't true. Wasn't true.

Julian!

It was Cassie's voice. From somewhere. From his own heart—the heart that pounded in his chest now—a defiant, fiery thing, willing him to stay alive. For Cassie, for Violeta.

There was only one way to stop the numbing chill from reaching his core. He must stoke the fire within himself that could never be extinguished. He closed his eyes and saw orange flame. Then the ripping began.

Julian had learnt over the years not to fight the way his body wanted to change. It had been painful at first, when he was resisting it, denying who he was. But today he welcomed the transformation and would have gladly embraced any pain for the lengthening and the strengthening, the way his back arched into shape, the way his coat covered him like black silk, and his teeth became the weapons he needed them to be.

The dog leapt at Thorne in a single, graceful arc, with a

speed and precision propelled by the deadly fury in the coiled-up springs of his muscles.

Thorne was dead within seconds.

The blood in Julian's mouth tasted vile. His claws slipped on the tiles as he turned towards the second man, who stood staring, horrified, by Alisa's side. The moment Julian locked eyes with him, he released her and raced away, and Julian had no wish to follow. Alisa started for the stairs and Julian loped down behind her, pausing in the next stairwell to melt back into his human form.

He found Alisa out on the street, bent double, her hands on her knees. He licked his dry lips and came to stand silently beside her. She straightened, her face pale, and wordlessly linked an arm around his. Numbness stole through him as he allowed her to lead him away from the office tower, away from the blood, away from Cassie.

16

The Darkweaver led Cassie to a door at the end of the corridor that opened into a bright office space with a floor to ceiling view over the rooftops and gardens of the city of Melbourne.

He directed her to two swivel lounge chairs facing each other across a round glass coffee table.

"Take a seat, please."

Cassie perched on the edge of a chair and crossed her legs. He flung himself into the other seat with elegant nonchalance, then sat forward, viewing her over folded fingers.

"It is quite delicious to meet you finally."

"You sound as if you're going to eat me."

He threw his head back and laughed, white teeth shining, golden hair shimmering in sunlight that danced around the room of its own accord, as though reflected many times over by invisible mirror globes.

"I can give you my utmost assurance that I don't eat people."

"No, just suck them dry," she said, looking squarely at him.

He made an unpleasant face. "You make it sound so distasteful, Cassandra."

"My name's Cassie."

"Cassie, then."

He stood up, strode across to an old-fashioned looking sideboard and poured himself a glass of something out of a ceramic pitcher.

"A drink?"

"No."

"While admittedly entertaining, wasting my power on that creature, your...boyfriend?"—his mouth turned down as though he'd tasted something sour—"gave me a thirst."

Cassie stared at him, so overtaken by the hot rage rising up within that she trembled with it. She wished fiercely, with the full force of her being, that she could smash her fist into the Darkweaver's face.

His eyes widened and he staggered back as though she really had hit him. Righting himself, his a hand at his cheek, his stunned expression soon darkened into a furious snarl.

"What," he ground out through clenched teeth, "was *that?*"

Cassie felt the surprise on her own face. "I...I don't know."

"No one has ever dared..."

He loomed over her, a menacing silhouette against the brilliant glare from the window, and hauled her up by her wrists. He stared hard at her. His breath smelt of aniseed; sweet and cold and syrupy. Then the lines around his jaw curved into a chilling smile.

"You really have no idea what power you have, do you? Or how to use it. You're like a child. Sit down." He shoved her back into the seat. "You have a lot to learn."

"I don't want to learn anything from you!"

He sniffed, his face a stony mask. "I am powerful and I am strong. But don't try me again, because I am not patient."

Cassie didn't move while he finished his drink, only followed him with her eyes as he opened a drawer in the desk. He lifted out what looked like a book or journal, bound in soft, worn leather. With a movement as efficient as a dancer's, he crossed to where Cassie sat, and dropped the book on the glass table in front of her.

"Your mother's."

Cassie reeled with surprise as he seated himself opposite her.

"Or should I say, *my sister's*."

"What?"

"Yes. And a very disappointed uncle I have been, that my dear sister has treated me so cruelly as to deprive me of the company of my own niece."

"Where is she? My mother. Have you done something to her?"

The Darkweaver laughed, sunlight sparking off his eyes. "Now why would I do that?"

Cassie sat very still, her heart leaping in its cage like a deer. "What about my father?"

The Darkweaver shrugged. "Honestly, I thought you were supposed to be clever. What would I want with your father?" His face was a sneer. "He is nothing, no one of import."

Cassie's fists clenched as rage rose within her again. He seemed to sense it this time though, because she felt a wall, invisible and impenetrable, draw up between them.

"Control yourself," he hissed.

His stare was brutal. Everything felt bright and hard. A desert under the sun. Breathe. Keep breathing.

"You are like her," he said eventually, uncrossing his legs and leaning forward to pick up the book. "Impulsive as the sea but predictable as its tides. You have her eyes. Such beautiful eyes. What colour would you say they are? Blue? Gold? Green? I love beautiful things, Cassie. And you are a beautiful thing."

She shuddered.

"Now, have a look at this." He opened the book to a page near the middle and slid it across the glass to her.

The left-hand side was filled with handwriting, and on the opposite page was drawn a fearsome-looking wolf or dog with its jaws wide, revealing sharp teeth dripping with something that, even though the picture was in black and white, looked horribly like blood.

"What's this?" She was ashamed to hear the fear in her voice.

His eyes glittered with dark amusement. "You don't know?"

"I don't know what you're talking about," she said, trying to read his face whose surreal beauty was so jarringly at odds with the malevolent expressions upon it.

"But they're your friends. Surely they would have told you?"

She knew she was walking into a baited trap, but her curiosity won out; it always had and always would. She wondered if he knew this about her. He already seemed to know a good deal more than she would have liked.

"Told me what?"

"Truly? You *are* alone, aren't you? No mother, no father, and not even your closest friends trust you enough to confide in you."

He flicked a wrist and the dancing sunlight died, as though he had trapped it within his palm, plunging them into darkness. Even the windows looked like grey mirrors upon whose surface shadowed shapes flickered.

Cassie gasped.

"That's right, my dear, they are correct to be afraid of you, right not to trust you. See what we can do? All the world is but shadow puppetry. They see only this. But you and I, we see so much more. Surely, you are not content to live your life in a simulacrum of reality? Pretending there is only this. This grey and ordinary life."

She heard his fingers click, and the room was once again flooded with warmth and golden light.

"Cassie. Sweet Cassie. Nothing is wrong. Nothing is forbidden." He reached for her hand.

She snatched it away, staring at him.

"I have also been alone." He stood up and walked across to the window. "Our dear mother did not believe that her blood ran as true in me as it did in her daughter. The gift does not often pass down to men, you see. Your mother received all the training, all the benefits of the collected knowledge of generations, all the admiration,"—he swung around to face her, sneering— "leaving me to scrabble in the dark, alone, poring over my mother's texts, teaching myself all I needed to know."

Cassie shivered. She couldn't help but see her own hands rummaging through her mother's drawer, finding the black book, hiding it under her bed, or feel the guilt, the sense of betrayal, as what she thought she knew of her mother shimmered like a mirage before her eyes.

He was smiling now, not at her, but into some imagined distance. "The beautiful irony is that I have become so much more powerful than your grandmother could ever have dreamt, so much more than your mother. And really, had I allowed myself to become shackled by their rules and codes, I would only ever have been a diminished being. I cannot deceive myself now that all that went before was not, in the end, for the best."

"So, you forgave her? Your mother...my grandmother?" Cassie asked, hearing her own voice in the silence: tentative, hopeful, childish.

To her surprise, he laughed; a glorious sound that brought the sunlight dancing around his head and down his body in long, glowing streamers.

"No, darling girl. I killed her."

ALISA AND JULIAN had made their way back to the hotel without speaking, but now that they were here, Alisa seemed to want to talk. She led Julian into the hotel's guest lounge off the foyer and sat him down by the crackling fire.

"Don't blame yourself, Julian."

Was it so easy for her to tell that he was doing just that? The grim kill, losing Cassie, the violent dousing of the last flame of hope that his mother was alive—all this was heavier on his heart than anything that had come before. He shook his head and glared at the flames. He *did* blame himself. For all of it.

No matter that he'd trained for it, that he'd promised himself he'd do whatever it took to find Violeta, he was not a born fighter, not a killer. Yet he had fought and killed. And he had also lost. Lost the one good thing he'd had left.

The flames danced in the grate, and he remembered another night when he had sat by an open fire, in the winter room at home, with his mother kneeling by his side, the smell of eucalyptus oil permeating the air as she squeezed warm water from a cloth and dabbed at a long cut across his back.

You need to be more careful, mi hijo querido.

He'd heard his father's car rolling up the drive that evening and had panicked, snagging himself on a low branch in his haste to return to human form. Mr Walcott had been away for the week, and Violeta had taken the opportunity to help Julian learn to control the Change; lessons, she'd said, that were long overdue. And they were—the unfamiliar surges of powerful emotions he'd been experiencing had made it more and more difficult to prevent an involuntary Change. He had run from his father and into the forest more times than he cared to count recently, which he knew only added to his view of him as a weakling and a coward.

The smell of blood and eucalyptus was making him queasy.

I don't want to hurt anyone, Mamá. What if I do?

She'd cast aside the wet cloth and clasped her hands either side of his shoulders.

You have the same choices you've always had. A strong man, a man who has a weapon handed to him, may yet choose to be peaceful. You are a Spiritwalker, not a monster. What you do with your strength and power remains your choice.

The iron smell of blood lingered as he turned to Alisa. A wash of hurt and shame and wrongness flooded through him. When had he become a man willing to hurt another? Would Violeta have the same faith in him now? How could he even look Cassie in the face again, knowing that he had ended a man's life? He'd wanted to tell Cassie what he was, almost *had* told her, so many times before. But now he knew he could not reveal the beast that he was to his dearest friend. He could justify the death all too easily. It had been self-defence; he was avenging his mother; Thorne had been a despicable human being. Yet, he had made the choice to do it, in that last moment when the heat of Thorne's blood had poured into his mouth and Julian hadn't let go. It had to have been his choice, because if it wasn't, then it was worse—it meant his mother had been wrong and he *was* a monster.

"Julian?"

He looked up at Alisa, knowing his pain was blazing, naked upon his face, and that it made him weak and the lesser for it.

"She asked us to wait for her." His voice sounded rough and imploring in his own ears.

Alisa met his eyes. "And we will."

"For how long? He could be doing anything to her!"

"He'd do worse to you, Julian. She's stronger than you know, than even she knows. You yourself said she could handle it."

"But we have to do something. Or do you suggest we lounge around here having hot showers and buffet breakfasts while she endures God knows what?" He kicked the solid leg of the coffee table in front of them, knowing he was being unfair. The orange jolt that seared through his foot was blinding, but it was a welcome pain.

Alisa shook her head. "While I do advocate for a hot shower, no, we don't sit around. We plan. The Dark Cross-Quarter is the day after tomorrow. It's our chance to find Tomas, find your mother. She may yet be alive. If any of what I've learnt over the last few years is true, then the Dark-weaver will also know this date. He may be waiting for this chance too, when the veil between the worlds is at its thinnest. Whatever his designs, this is as much his best chance to enter the word between worlds as it is ours. I believe we have an assignation with this man. Cassie will surely be with him. We just need to discover where to be when the time is right. Where is our Miles Cross?"

Her words flowed over and around Julian as though he

were a rock in a river. None of it went in, none of it made sense. A bone-deep exhaustion had overtaken him, and he could do very little other than stare glassily at the licking tongues of the fire.

Eventually, he dragged himself upstairs. Alisa had wanted to order dinner to their rooms, but he'd waved away her offer. There was no place for food in his knotted stomach. He showered in a daze. Even the hot water and soap couldn't wash away the dread, or the memory of blood. Later, he lay on the bed in the dark, concentrating on the muted traffic sounds outside his window and the quiet hum of the fridge. He needed to stay awake, because to sleep would be to close the day on Cassie, to give up on her. He would get up and go for a walk, keep the night from closing in. But his weary body stubbornly disobeyed his commands. The gold-flecked sea of Cassie's eyes was all he saw as he finally surrendered to sleep.

JULIAN WAS ALREADY AWAKE, dressed and pacing by the time Alisa appeared in the foyer. The look she gave him was wary. He watched her square her shoulders before walking up to him. She was such a slight thing, reaching only up to his collar bone, but she took a firm hold of his arm.

"Food first." She guided him towards the hotel restaurant. "I'll meet you in there in a moment. I need a quick chat with Maree."

With a little nudge of encouragement from Alisa, he pushed open the door and immediately regretted it. The greasy odour of fried breakfast foods was an assault, and he wanted nothing more in that moment than to be back in the Curwood, breathing the fresh scent of eucalyptus and cold night air. Fighting back nausea, he found a seat by the window. From here he could see Alisa through the glass panel in the door, talking with the lady at the front desk.

Soft sunlight flooded in through the sheer mesh curtains, setting the white tablecloth and cutlery glowing. He shivered, despite the warmth and light. *Cassie*. Where had she slept the night? Had she slept at all? Surely, he would know if something terrible had happened to her. Wouldn't he?

The waiter, the young man from the night before, a night so long ago, was leaning over, asking what he wanted. Julian shook his head and the boy mercifully left him alone.

Alisa burst through the door a moment later, followed by an imposing, curvy woman. Her hair was set in deep, red curls; several long necklaces layered the florid skin of her chest and flowed down over a burnt-orange dress—an ensemble that gave the impression she was a living flame.

"This is Maree," Alisa said, pulling out two chairs from around the table. "She owns the hotel." She turned to Maree. "I'm so glad we've finally got a chance to talk to you."

Maree flashed a smile at them both. "Yes!" Then she rolled her eyes. "I've been away. What a palaver! Takes more work having a holiday than staying here, I swear."

Alisa turned to Julian. "I chose this place for us because Maree is Cassie's aunt."

"Wow. Okay."

"It's been years since I've seen Cassie," said Maree, now frowning deeply. "I do hope she's all right. I no longer have anything to do with my brother, but I remember what he is capable of."

"Your brother?" Julian asked, confused.

"Anything you can tell us," prompted Alisa, who had obviously already digested this new detail during her earlier talk with Maree and was now like a bloodhound with a scent, "might be the information we need to help Cassie."

Maree's labile face brightened and she leaned forward conspiratorially. "I could give you a little history about the original Spiritweaver family we're descended from."

"We'd love to hear it," urged Alisa, though from the shining look of Maree's eyes now, she clearly needed very little in the way of encouragement.

"I don't know where we're from originally, but I know the family came out here in the late 1800s." Maree spoke animatedly, but also quietly enough that nearby patrons couldn't hear her words.

"When my predecessors first arrived in Victoria they sought out local Weavers. It took a lot of time and a lot of listening to learn how it worked in this country, to build relationships and to earn trust." She paused, looking around, her tongue flicking out over her lips.

"And even as my family was establishing themselves in the city, learning the ways, colonial authorities were draining the last of Melbourne's wetlands." Her rings flashed as she plucked at the corner of a napkin. "The Yarra River, Birrarung, was choked and dying, its course redirected, and all its billabongs silted up and paved over."

"Birrarung." The ancient Woiwurrung name rolled across Julian's tongue like flowing water. His father had loved old maps of Melbourne, but it had been Violeta who had read to him about the city's history, had inspired him to explore the living layers beneath those maps. "*River of mists and shadows.*"

Maree nodded, but the smile she gave him was sorrowful. "Indeed." Her fingers smoothed the tablecloth.

They were silent until Maree began to speak again, her voice a bitter hiss. "The largest remaining swamp became ringed by slaughterhouses and eventually drained. It was no longer a place for Walkers or Weavers, at least not for Earth-weavers. No place to guard the boundary between the worlds. It became more to a Darkweaver's liking, with plenty of its own, man-made devils."

The reception bell chimed. Maree looked up as if shaking herself out of a dream, and the bright, animated smile snapped back into place. "Ah, new guests. I have to go. You two enjoy your breakfast now. Food's on the house while you're under my roof. Keep me posted on my niece."

She pushed her chair back and Alisa stood up too. They exchanged hugs and Maree hurried away through the swinging door to reception.

"Is Maree a Spiritweaver then?" Julian asked Alisa once she'd gone.

Alisa shook her head. "What are you going to eat?" she said, watching the waiter make his way across the room to their table.

"Nothing."

"A cappuccino and an orange juice please, and two servings of the Big Breakfast," she ordered briskly, before the boy had even taken out his pad.

"You'll eat," she commanded, once the waiter had left, casting Julian a steely look. "If not for yourself, for Cassie."

Julian shrugged, but his stomach grumbled traitorously.

"Anyway, no, she doesn't count herself as a Weaver," Alisa continued, "although she has a small amount of power, so in reality, she *is* one. Her mother was a powerful Earthweaver. And her daughter, Selene...she's like us."

Julian dropped the fork he'd been fiddling with. "What?"

"She can Change, Julian. Like you and me."

"But that means—" He regarded her, his eyes widening.

"That Selene's father was a Spiritwalker, yes. I haven't

heard that there's a law against Weavers and Walkers falling in love. And clearly, it happens from time to time."

He looked down, feeling Alisa'a scrutinising gaze on him, his heart thudding so loudly he was sure she could hear it. He twisted the fork against the tablecloth, directing a beam of sunlight into his eyes. "What's her spirit animal? The daughter's?"

"A fox, I believe."

What must it be like living this way in the city? At home, it had been so easy to be fully himself in the forest, night or day, with little care that someone might see him or try to trap or poison him. He guessed there must be foxes living in Melbourne already, but surely it would make things harder to live in a city, which never truly slept, where there were always people about, and few wild spaces to roam. He wondered where the fox daughter was now.

Then, as a magnet returns to its natural pole, his thoughts turned to Violeta. To the night she had returned to him, not long after his father's farce of a memorial, and how her soft howling beneath his window had woken him from a desolate nightmare. To the way he felt his heart had been returned to him when he realised she'd escaped her captor, that his mother was alive. And how she had kept her distance from his father, living up in the mountains above them, fearing to return lest she once again provoke John Walcott's anger and revulsion. How he had loved their wild races together through the forest, the peaceful times in the secret sunny glade, when there had been no need to explain or to fear, no need to be other than who they were.

"Julian." Alisa was leaning forward.

He tried to focus on her, but his mother's face shimmered before him, blocking all sound and vision. "What did you say?"

"I said, I'm going to see Nellie this afternoon. Find out if she has any ideas about where we need to be tomorrow."

"Tomorrow?"

Alisa gave him a look that was half exasperated, half soft with concern. "Yes, tomorrow, for the Cross-Quarter."

17

*C*assie awoke on her knees. She'd been in a forest under a sky bright with stars. Running; branches lashing her skin, hot breath on her heels, yellow teeth and hunter's eyes. Now she was awake. The floor was warm, like a living skin beneath her. She pulled herself to her feet and made her way around the bed to the window. It wasn't yet dawn. The room looked out over a sea of orange lights; the city's luminous canopy, extending to the horizon in a fretwork of buildings and highways. Like the work of a Darkweaver. A city burning with stolen power.

The room the Darkweaver had locked her in had the clean, bright feel of a modern hotel, with a sofa bed made up with a simple white coverlet, a side table and a small bathroom. It was almost possible to imagine she really was a guest here, like he'd said as he'd led her down this corridor the night before, asking what she liked best to eat and what clothes she favoured. She'd given him no answers, but as soon as he'd bolted the door, food had materialised on the side table and clothing on the bed, laid out in a neat row.

She'd gulped down the water and devoured a sandwich, but had tossed the clothes aside and crawled into the bed. Closing her eyes hadn't been her intention, but within minutes, she'd willingly embraced the numbing elixir of sleep.

Now, in the silence, looking out at the headlights of cars and the glow of apartment windows, she felt incredibly alone. She wanted her parents. That this man could claim to be her uncle sickened her, turning everything that family meant to her inside out. There was nothing of her mother in him. And even the sting of hidden truths she felt now alongside the glowing place in her heart reserved for Lyra, even that was but a pinprick alongside the roiling in her stomach at the thought of her captor, her so-called uncle. And wondering why he might want her here, what good he thought she could be to him, disturbed her even more.

As the sky lightened, Cassie locked herself in the bathroom and took a shower, hoping the heat might melt some of the ice that seemed to have lodged inside her chest. The water did little good, but at least she was no longer shivering. She pulled on her jeans. Her top was filthy; something cleaner and warmer to wear could not be a bad thing. She inspected the clothes she'd shoved aside the night before. Amongst the pile was a silvery grey t-shirt and a sea-green sweater of soft, fine wool. They both fit perfectly, which was disquieting. She put the star necklace back on. If she concentrated, she could almost imagine its gentle press against her skin was her mother's reassuring touch.

The clouds outside the window were pink with sunrise and the city had a faded, barely awake feeling, grey with the lost brilliance of streetlights. The leafless trees lining empty streets were mournful against the bland buildings, and even the slow-crawling silver trams seemed listless.

It was almost imperceptible at first, but the longer she stared at the bleak cityscape before her, the less distinct she felt from all that was outside the glazed window. The starflower grew warm above her heart and then it began to pulse. It was subtle; the feel of distant forest drums, but soon it grew into a more insistent bass, a thrumming like water pulling back from a rocky shoreline before the next crashing wave. The drumming was both within her and without; it was her blood pounding through her veins, the tides of water inside her. Her skin was a drum, her bones beat the rhythm and her heart was its pulse. Nothing in her was separate from the heartbeat of the world. She need only pull one thread, feel its resonance, shift and weave, a tweak here, half a turn there, and the dance would be made. She turned, vibrating and spinning until the weaving was done.

The cold was the first thing to hit her. Then the ground. She opened her eyes. Bare-limbed branches threaded across a pale sky. For a moment, the world was still. After that came pain. She cried out and rolled onto her side, drawing her knees to her chest as fire lanced up and down her arms, her legs. She wanted to scream with the burning, but every breath was like a brand to her heart. Gasping and writhing, digging her nails into her palms, aware only that she was losing some battle, that soon everything would be dark, the agony abruptly ceased. She rolled onto her back in relief, drawing in gulps of air, her face wet with tears, her hands slippery with blood.

It was minutes before she could finally sit up and get her bearings. She was in a small park with wrought iron benches and grass strewn with orange leaves. There was not a soul about. Surrounding the park was a narrow road, a ring of brick townhouses, and behind them, a series of high-rise buildings. One building was immediately recognisable—the silver monolith with the locked room that had held her only moments ago. She scrambled to her feet. The pain had subsided to a hollow ache in her chest. What had she done? How had she done it? The starflower was cool now, as though it was nothing more than a simple pendant. She tucked it beneath her sweater with shaking hands and made her way across the drifts of fallen leaves to a path that led out of the park and onto the street, desiring only to be out from under the gaze of the Darkweaver's office tower as quickly as possible.

She stared down at her feet as she walked. Who was to say that they would touch the footpath and not fall straight through it? Or that they wouldn't whisk her to another spot? It was a dizzying feeling, this lack of certainty in something she had taken for granted: that the world was solid, that time and space followed rules she knew in her every primordial cell. Could she even call what she had just accomplished 'magic'? It seemed so small a word for it, trite even. Whatever had just occurred was much more like a ripping and reweaving of the fabric of the universe. It wasn't some trick; it was something as far removed from the idea of wands and words as she could imagine. She had reshaped reality. The face of Tomas's sister, the physics major with the long dark hair and thoughtful eyes, came to her mind. This was cosmology. This was dynamics and forces, space and time. *The language of the Universe, Cassie.*

It took her some time to navigate the maze of town-houses and small laneways until she found a main street that she recognised. From here, she was almost sure she could find her way back to the hotel. She'd begun to hurry, walking fast, when she saw it; a dark shadow at the corner of her eye, a feeling of something huge, flattened against the wall of a laneway, regarding her, following her along the busy street.

Then, like a snuffed flame, the feeling, or whatever it was, simply vanished. She shivered. Who knew what side-effects there were of what she had just done? She hoped that hallucinations were the worst of it. She rubbed a hand over her chest where the last remnant of the burning feeling was lifting from her like smoke.

It was a relief finally to reach the hotel. She raced up the steps and burst into the lobby, startling a red-haired lady at the front desk, whose eyes widened as Cassie ran up to her.

"Hi, I'm Cassie. I have a room here. Well, I hope I still do. I'm with Alisa."

The woman stood up, covering her mouth with her hands. She had lovely eyes, hazel with flecks of gold, a lot like her mother's.

"Cassie! Oh, I'm glad to see you." She came out from behind the desk and brought Cassie's hands into her own.

"I'm Maree," she said in answer to Cassie's widened eyes. "Your aunt. You won't remember me," she continued quickly. "You would have been too young the last time Lyra brought you here. We've been so worried about you."

Cassie took a step back. Maree released her with a look of concern.

"I'm sorry," said Cassie, once she'd found her voice, "it's just, I didn't know I had an aunt. I've just met an uncle I didn't know about, and he wasn't exactly a pleasant sort."

Maree's eyes met hers, the kindly light in them abruptly shadowed, her shoulders taut and angled inwards as she breathed: "Dominic."

"Dominic," Cassie spoke the name with a sour taste in her mouth. "He wouldn't tell me his name."

Maree nodded solemnly. "That sounds about right." She sighed. "Please believe me. I am nothing like him."

Cassie nodded warily. "So how many other brothers and

sisters did Mum have that I didn't know about. Or are you Dad's sister?"

Maree gave her a sad little smile. "No, I am Lyra's sister. It was just me, your mother and Dominic."

"So why—"

"Why haven't I been in your life?"

"Yeah, I guess."

"Your mother and I had a disagreement when you were a baby. About our brother, actually. When our mother...died...Lyra wanted nothing to do with Dominic. She blamed him. I wasn't so sure. I wanted to give him the benefit of the doubt. I was wrong. I know that now, but it caused a rift between us."

"He told me he killed her, your mother," said Cassie, suddenly weary to her bones.

Maree nodded. "Yes. As I said, I was wrong. It was hard for me to let the idea of who my little brother was die too. Your mother always saw him more clearly than I, who was closer to him in age." She blinked and shook her head. "You are very tired. Go upstairs and make yourself at home. Rest. The others aren't here. They went out this morning, I'm not sure where."

Cassie swallowed.

Maree gave her a motherly pat on the shoulder. "Let me know when you need something; food, anything, and I'll have it made up for you. If you feel like a chat at any time, just ring this bell. It must be very scary for you not knowing what has happened to your parents and then meeting Dominic. I'm just glad you're safe."

Her mother's eyes, but not her mother. Cassie nodded and looked away. It was suddenly all too much. The malice of the man who proclaimed himself her uncle, the tenderness of this woman who claimed she was her aunt, the tangle of real and unreal, familiar and alien; it all made for a confused mind and a sense of heaviness that in this moment felt almost impossible to bear.

"Thank you," was all she could manage, and under Maree's sympathetic scrutiny, she stumbled up the staircase to her room.

The first thing Cassie did was try to call her parents. But again, neither answered their phones, though she held until the mocking dial-tone went dead. She crossed to the glass doors and drew them roughly aside. Frigid autumn air pierced the overheated room. The traffic noise was like a conversation, the revs of the cars, a hollow echo where they sped past the brick building across the street, a disappointed slowing at the clicking pedestrian crossing to her left. Where were Ali and Julian? Down amongst that purposeful flow somewhere, no doubt. Waiting for them was clearly the sensible course of action, but sense and patience were not virtues that were whispering to her now.

She leaned over the balcony, half hoping she might glimpse a fox amongst the cars and people. She would have liked to talk with Selene again, who she now realised must be her cousin. But it was no flicker of orange that caught her eye. It was something else. Something huge and black, plastered against the underside of Julian's balcony, edging towards her. Cassie shrieked and drew back, but not before she'd caught sight of the dark thing moving, as fluidly and quietly as a shadow, from Julian's balcony to her own, wraithlike arms reaching and pulling; for all the world like an enormous spider fashioned out of soot.

She stumbled into her room, slammed the sliding doors closed and locked them quickly. She wanted to move, to flee, but her legs wouldn't obey her, and she could only watch, her eyes widening, mouth opening in horror, as the thing rose like black smoke on her balcony.

It turned in a half circle, and what had seemed an insubstantial black miasma was now solid flesh: a spider's abdomen, dragging and bouncing in a repulsive and decidedly real way across the stone. Cassie gasped, tears springing to her eyes. She tried to call out, but only a thin wail of fear escaped her mouth. The thing turned to face her. Where the spider's many-eyed head should have been was the pale face of a woman with straight dark hair, eyes as black as two pits, and lips the red of congealed blood.

Cassie Drake.

Even as her heart pounded in her chest, a prisoner desperate for escape, she noted that the spider-woman's mouth was not moving. Instead, Cassie felt and heard the words in her mind. The black eyes seemed to look directly at her, though with no whites around the pupils, it was hard to be completely sure. Their expression was impossible to discern.

I can smell your mother's blood in your veins.

Cassie shivered, but although she wished fiercely to step back from the glass, her legs seemed to have turned to stone.

You fear me. There is no need to fear me. Your blood is my blood. All Spiritweavers are my daughters and my sons.

Cassie tried to move her mouth, to form words, but nothing came.

I wish only to warn you. Be discerning in your reweaving of the web. You are untrained, unschooled in the etiquette of such things. For that I forgive you. The Woven is a fine and balanced thing. You have a responsibility to what is, as much as to what could be. Do not use your gifts unwisely or with abandon.

Cassie lowered her head and managed a nod. When she

looked up, the dark eyes were still watching her, as though waiting for more of an assurance.

She licked her dry lips. "I understand. I will be more...discerning in the future. I am sorry."

After a long moment of stillness, the creature seemed satisfied and made to turn towards the edge of the balcony.

"Wait!"

It paused, the unfathomable face turning towards her again.

"Who *are* you?"

Cassie could almost imagine she saw amusement in the creature's face.

I am she of many names. I have been called the Great Goddess, Neith, Uttu, Iktomi, Ishtar, Arachne. And many more. I have my favourites, but you may choose your own.

Cassie opened her mouth to speak again, but the Spider Goddess began turning on the spot, becoming a dark blur as she spun faster and faster until, with a silver flash, she vanished.

It was several moments before Cassie regained the use of her legs, and even then, she stood rooted, staring at the point in space where the spider being had vanished. Then she began to shiver, and a wave of numbing exhaustion washed through her so that it was all she could do to stagger to the bed and collapse upon it. As she lay staring up at the ceiling with cold running up and down her body and sweat beading on her forehead as though she had a fever, a small, distant part of her mused that there must be a limit to the amount of weirdness one mind could take in a day. She closed her eyes.

⁓

A SOFT KNOCK at the door startled her awake. She hadn't been aware of falling asleep, but the light in the room had faded to dull afternoon shadows and the sky outside was heavy and grey. The knock came again. She staggered to her feet and opened the door.

It was Julian. Her heart gave an approving thump in her chest. Julian, nudging a lock of dark hair out of his eyes with his shoulder instead of his hands because he was carrying a bowl of food. Food! Thick wedges of roast potato sprinkled with rough-cut salt, whose savoury smell set her mouth watering.

"You might just be the most beautiful thing I have seen, ever!" she said, snatching the bowl from him and pulling him inside.

She gave a squeak of surprise as he drew her into a crushing hug.

"I thought we'd lost you," he said into her hair.

She pulled back. His cheeks were russet with heightened colour and his pupils were large and dark. There was an unaccustomed openness on his face, a fierceness in his eyes.

"Julian." She set the bowl down unevenly on the table behind her.

What could she tell him? How to explain the inexplicable? It almost hurt to feel him watching her, intense and searching as though for a wound, if not on her skin, then within her soul. She pressed her lips together and avoided his eyes. "I'm okay."

He shoved his hands into his pockets.

"Better eat them before they get cold then." He indicated the potato wedges with his chin.

He seemed transfixed for a moment by the sinuous band of steam rising from the bowl. When he looked back at her, his face had closed like a fan.

She pulled out a chair and sat down, hugging her knees to her chest. She'd seen him in full colour for a moment, a mere sliver of time. How long had he been a black and white version of himself? And why hadn't she realised it until now?

He remained hovering by the door.

"Join me?"

He hesitated, then seated himself in the chair opposite.

"Where's Ali?" she asked.

"Downstairs, talking with Maree." He gestured towards the door. "I didn't realise she was your aunt."

"Neither did I until today." She pushed the bowl towards him. "Julian, I'm sorry." He looked startled. "I was so worried that he wouldn't let you go, that I'd made a horrible mistake leaving you both."

He looked at her in disbelief. "*You* leaving *us*? We left *you*. When you walked down that corridor with him, Cassie...I've never felt so scared." He swallowed.

"The Darkweaver's name is Dominic. He killed his own mother. My grandmother. He says he's my uncle. What does that make me?"

Julian frowned. "It doesn't make you anything," He leaned forward. "He defines nothing about you."

She looked to the window, as though the crack of sky above the buildings held an answer. For once, she didn't feel childish. In fact, she didn't feel young at all, but strangely old and weary.

"Cas, how did you get out of there?"

It was the question she least knew how to answer. The sun dropped below a bank of steel clouds and sent golden beams into the room like shafts of sunlight angling into a forest—a forest the way the Curwood had been that afternoon she and Ali had walked home from the Walcott's property, a lifetime ago now. She shivered and found herself drawing closer to Julian.

"Truthfully, I don't know. I used...magic, I guess. Only it wasn't like anything I've done before." She stopped short of telling him about the visitation from the Spider Goddess, if that was what she was, and not an invention of her own mind.

"Cassie, you're amazing. The things you can do."

Julian's eyes gleamed like polished wood. The light illuminated his face, picking out the angles, turning him from gold to bronze.

She selected a wedge of potato, not wanting him to see the flush that was rising, unbidden, to her cheeks.

She took a bite. The outside was salty and crunchy, and inside, it was warm and smooth against her tongue.

Her eyes were drawn back to his face. He was regarding her with an unusually soft, glassy look. She pushed the bowl towards him and he leaned across and picked out a piece. For a full minute, they did nothing but eat, their eyes on the food. The taste and the sharp awareness of her hunger almost drove everything else away. Almost.

She was studiously collecting the last grains of salt in the bowl when he stood up. His quick movement startled her.

"I should go tell Ali you're okay."

"Wait." She stood too. "I'll come with you."

His hands tightened on the back of the chair, but he nodded. "I'll meet you out on the landing."

She ducked into the bathroom and splashed water on her face. It surprised her that she looked pale in the mirror given the fire that was coursing through her. The starflower lay against her chest, quiet as glass, but she tucked it beneath her jumper anyway, unsure of whether Maree would approve of her having it.

JULIAN GRIPPED THE RAILING, sweat beading down his back, heat ripping through his core. His ears had the ringing, rushing sound they got just before a Change, when his blood roared like a great sea in the thrall of a massive object, pulled to a new state of being as though by a king tide.

But it wasn't a Change coming, he understood this now, for the first time. Fear had bound him in its blind panic, but with her here, safely behind that door, he understood the difference. Now he could see through the dark water to something glowing; and this gleaming thing was the precious knowledge that she, Cassie, was the cause of this new tide within him. This falling towards her was not a signal of a Change, but something older, something all creatures knew, what the entire Universe knew—attraction: that bending of space and time, of beingness, towards another who burned brighter.

Her door opened.

"Cassie." How weirdly formal he sounded. "Shall we go down?"

She joined him against the banister and closed her fingers gently over his right hand.

"Not yet." He didn't dare move for fear she'd let him go. "First tell me. Have I done something to hurt you?"

He could barely breathe. "No. You've never hurt me." His voice felt rough and his words caught in his throat. "You've never given me anything but more and more cause to—"

He stopped himself. Whatever this was, this new attention from his lifelong friend, this energy between them, he didn't want to be the one to break it, to scare her away. He carefully turned his hand in hers so that their palms were touching and brought his gaze to her face.

A tiny frown appeared between her eyebrows, the one she got when she was looking down to read, or concentrating hard, or when something confused her.

"To what?"

He could see the small holes in her earlobes where she'd worn earrings as a kid. He remembered the colourful, dangling loops against her neck. Now, as she stood watching him, neither of them children anymore, he saw his own face reflected in her extraordinary eyes. The dark fan of her eyelashes brushed her cheek as she blinked. Her lips were pink and soft. He leaned closer, and she moved into the space between them until there was none.

Their mouths touched, and even as he kissed her, tasted the salt and sweetness of her mouth, he could hardly bring himself to believe that it was real, that she was here, wanting him as much as he had always wanted her. He pulled her close, pressing her to him as though they could become one being. He found her jawline, kissed along it, down her neck, across the cool gold of her necklace to her collarbone. She was holding him as though he were her lifeboat. He wished that he was, willed that he could be, but he was with her in the same, roiling sea.

A sound from below the landing sent them rocketing apart from one another. Footsteps, someone climbing the stairs towards them. She straightened her sweater, patting the starflower beneath it. They looked at one another. He saw her dilated pupils, the pulse at her throat, and knew he must look the same. He touched his palm to her cheek and felt her smile beneath his hand.

"Come on," she said to him, "it's probably Ali."

18

*I*t wasn't Ali. Still reeling from the feel of Julian's mouth on hers, it took Cassie a moment to recognise that the young girl dashing up the stairs towards them was Selene.

"Cassie!" The fox-girl looked wild. She grasped Cassie's hand. "Quick, we have to go!

She shot Julian a wary glance and sniffed at the air. Her eyes narrowed as she tugged at Cassie.

"He can come too if he wants, but we have to hurry. Come on."

Selene pulled Cassie not down the stairs, but past their rooms to a door in the wall at the very end of the corridor.

"Pull!" Selene ordered Julian, and he lunged forward and tugged at the door.

It opened onto a fire escape. Cold air sliced through Cassie's jumper. "Where are we going? What about Ali? We can't just leave her!"

Selene jumped out onto a platform of square steel grating. "Just follow me."

"I'm going back to tell Ali."

"No!" snapped Selene. "Ali's not here. Mum said. Come on, we must leave. Now!"

Julian gave Cassie a mystified shrug and leapt onto the platform. Cassie shook her head and stepped out to join him.

They raced downstairs in single file, hanging onto the icy railing so as not to slip on the slick metal. As soon as they neared ground level, Selene leapt from the steps and streaked off along the pavement.

"Selene, slow down!" Cassie shouted.

"No time!" she called back, plunging into traffic and weaving her way to the other side of the road.

They raced across the road after her with cars blaring horns at them, chasing the red-headed blur through the maze of city streets.

Finally, they burst out onto a familiar green lawn leading down to the bridge across the river. This time though, the fox-girl didn't stop, but headed straight for the bluestone tunnel under the bridge.

They followed her into the dank half-light. Soon they could hear only a dull roar of traffic above them. As they ventured further in, the darkness became like a blanket. Even the traffic noise ceased. The only sound they could hear was their own breathing and the faint scraping of Selene's footsteps ahead of them. Cassie squeezed Julian's hand, and he squeezed back.

"Selene?" Cassie's voice echoed mutely in the long, narrow space.

"I'm here! Keep coming. It'll be light in a minute."

The smooth floor of the tunnel was wetter beneath their feet now, and Cassie could hear a tinkling, trickling sound. Water running down the walls? Or was it seeping along the rock beneath them? Although she could no longer see Julian, she could hear his breathing and smell the warm-earth, sweet-spice scent of him. The strength of his presence in this enclosed space made her head spin.

The next moment, the tunnel opened out into a wider cavern. Selene had been right, it *was* lighter. But not with daylight. All across the moist walls and high ceiling were bright green pinpoints of light, glimmering together so that the entire cavern glowed.

"Are they glow-worms?" she asked Selene in wonder.

Though it was still too dark to make out facial expressions, they could see her shaking her head.

"No. They're fungi. Beautiful, aren't they?"

Cassie remembered the multicoloured mushrooms that had blossomed at her feet and a new wariness welled up within her.

"Selene, where are we exactly?"

She was leading them through the cavern now towards a dark narrowing in the far wall and didn't answer.

Julian found Cassie's hand again in the darkness.

"You can call me Toto if you'd like," he whispered.

Cassie laughed. No one expected Julian to be funny. He let so little show on his face, especially these days, but she had always valued his wry take on the world, his gentle poking at things he rated absurd, and his fierce, quiet intelligence. It was only now that she was beginning to see the intensity beneath it all, the place where all his feelings roiled around like a storm and his passion to care for what he loved was rooted.

Selene stopped at the narrow entrance to the new tunnel, allowing them to catch up.

"Are you going to tell us what we're doing down here?" asked Cassie.

"Grandma says you'll be safer here. The Darkweaver is

angry with you for what you did, Cassie. He's looking for you right now. You must come with me."

"Selene," Cassie tried to keep her tone as neutral as possible, "when you say 'Grandma', do you mean Maree's mother? My grandma too?"

"Yes," said Selene, looking confused, "of course."

Cassie's glance flickered to meet Julian's briefly before she turned back to her cousin. "Because our grandmother is...no longer alive. So...how is it you are talking with her?"

Selene cocked her head to one side. "Grandma told me you were smart."

Cassie let out an exasperated breath.

"Of course she's dead," said Selene, "but she was a Spiritweaver, and I am her granddaughter. If you're strong in the Weaving, death is only an inconvenience. And Grandma was strong. She can still communicate with me when she needs to. And I can hear her when I want to."

"Could she, you know, come back to us if she wanted to?" asked Julian.

Selene shook her head, and the points of light on the wall behind her shimmered through her hair. "No. Well, maybe. But she respects the Woven too much to do that."

The uncanny face of the Spider Goddess filled Cassie's mind. The Woven. That which already is. It made a deep sense in her gut, and she had an inkling then of why she might have felt so much pain after shifting the threads that had bound her current reality. Perhaps that was the price she'd had to pay for causing such a drastic change in the Woven. A pang of frustration flashed inside her—she knew so little! It was her mother's fault. How could she have left her so untrained, so vulnerable? An unaccustomed anger with Lyra bubbled up in her heart. Anger at all the times her mother could have said something, anything to Cassie, about the power they both shared, and for all the times Cassie had missed her and wanted her near. What if they never had that chance again? The anger morphed into a cold wedge of fear that constricted her heart.

"Cas?" Julian's warm hand found her shoulder.

She took a deep breath and nodded. "All right, Selene. Lead on then."

If it was possible, the narrow fissure they followed her into felt even darker than the tunnel had. She could see nothing ahead of her, not even her own hand when she waved it in front of her face. She only knew that Julian was behind her by the soft scuffing of his shoes. She couldn't hear Selene at all. At least it wasn't as wet here. There was no water beneath their feet, and the few times she touched the cave wall to reorient herself, it felt cold and waxy beneath her fingers.

It had been several minutes, and Cassie was about to call out to her cousin when she noticed a soft glow from somewhere up ahead. As they walked on, the light became brighter until they could see Selene silhouetted in front of a square of light that seemed to be holding back a swirl of silver and grey smoke.

"Is this a Weaver Gate?" she whispered, watching the mesmerising patterns with awe.

Cassie heard Julian's intake of breath as he pulled up short behind her.

"Yes," said Selene. "Come on."

Selene reached her fingers into the base of the oscillating square of light, pulling it up as though it were a piece of canvas, and ushered them through beneath her upstretched arms.

Cassie stepped into the swirling light, and immediately, an acrid smoky tang shot up her nose and she felt her body being tugged from within, spun around and spat out. She landed heavily, dizzy and coughing, on a broad lawn of velvety moss, silvery green and spongy beneath her hands. A moment later, Julian appeared beside her. He rolled over onto all fours, coughing, as a fox appeared through the shimmering swirl of smoke, landing lightly behind him.

The spinning sensation worsened to nausea as she watched Selene revolve and shift from a fox into a human girl in front of her.

Cassie groaned. "I don't think I'm ever going to get used to that mode of travel."

Julian's face was pale with shock, his eyes dark and round. But it was Cassie he was staring at, not the fox who had just turned into a girl in front of his eyes.

"It's easier if you Change first," said Selene brightly.

Cassie felt her lungs squeeze but resisted another cough for fear she might vomit. "Yeah, well, that won't help us will it?"

Selene's eyebrows flickered, and she gave Julian a long look.

Julian brushed himself off and got to his feet, ignoring the look.

Cassie wondered at this exchange. Was Selene wary of Julian? Or curious?

"This way," said Selene in a tone that sounded neither wary nor curious to Cassie.

Julian rolled his shoulders back and straightened up. "Yes ma'am."

Selene jutted out her pointy little jaw and marched off across the moss. Cassie stifled a laugh, glancing at Julian, but he was already hurrying after Selene.

Cassie followed in a bewildered daze, her attention drawn

to a hundred micro details of their new world, this 'bubble', as Ali would have described it. The air was warm enough that she removed her jumper and tied it around her waist, but she couldn't locate the source of the warmth. There seemed to be a glow to the place, as though the sun was setting not just in the west, but on every part of the horizon, in all directions.

They crossed the moss lawn and passed through a copse of thin trees whose trunks were covered with lacy, blue lichen, before emerging onto a vast plain of low, tussocky grass. As they walked into the yellow swathe, Cassie could see that the grass was undulating as though moved by oceanic currents or winds she couldn't feel.

They walked along a narrow track, with hard clay beneath a surface of grey sand that gleamed with shimmering ripples with each step they took. Cassie was mesmerised by the glistening oscillations and patterns that rolled out behind Julian's shoes and joined up with hers as she walked.

"Cas!" Julian paused in front of her.

She looked up. Ahead of them, to their right, stood a bent and weathered tree trunk, silver with age and tilted at an angle, as if blown to the side by the force of a gale. As they drew nearer, they could see that the leaning portion of the trunk had a face. It was tempting to think someone had carved it into the wood, but Cassie knew enough of woodcarving from her dad to know that no one could have created such a lifelike rendering. The frozen expression was one of surprise, its eyes and mouth open and staring.

Cassie shivered.

"Look! There's another one." Julian pointed down the track.

Selene had stopped, finally, and was looking up at the

second frozen tree. When they caught up to her, they realised she was staring directly into its petrified eyes.

"They were my friends," she said, her face white.

"You knew them?" Cassie couldn't quite keep the disbelief out of her voice.

Selene nodded furiously and swiped at her cheeks. "I hate him!"

To Cassie's surprise, Julian crossed to Selene's side and laid a hand on her shoulder. "He won't get away with this."

Another long shiver snaked down Cassie's spine as she thought of the Darkweaver. *Nothing is wrong. Nothing is forbidden.*

They hurried along the path with their heads down after that. Selene directed them to the right at a fork and the track evened out again as the grass became dotted with grey boulders, then with larger piles of rock, and finally, small hillocks made entirely of granite tors slanting against one another.

Selene found a little track that led up one of these hills. The grass here was shorter and scattered densely with wildflowers; patches of vermillion giving way to white and yellow, and smaller sprinklings of purple in amongst a darker green as they ascended the hill. Finally, Selene led them through a crack between two towering boulders which opened out below them into a wide, grassy amphitheatre ringed by tors like a fortress. White flowers threaded through the grass at its centre, and bright green ferns lined all the cracks in the granite walls.

They clambered down after the fox-girl, stopping when she crouched in front of a hollow beneath a small pile of rocks and pulled out something wrapped in a red tea towel. She waved for them to join her on the grass and unwrapped the bundle to reveal a loaf of something that looked like sweet bread or cake. She tore some off for each of them.

"We can rest now. This is a safe place," she said.

Cassie took a bite. "Banana bread?"

Selene smiled, looking for once like the child she was. "Mum made it. It's my favourite."

Julian only nibbled a corner of his piece and looked around with a frown. "So, what's the plan?"

"We stay here," said Selene, pulling out cups and a canister of water from her hiding place in the rocks. She passed a full cup to Cassie.

"Thanks." Cassie guzzled down the water.

"For how long?" asked Julian, accepting his cup but not drinking from it.

"Until after the Cross-Quarter Alisa told you about. Which is tomorrow, in your world."

"What? No."

"We have to. It's not safe to be anywhere else until we know the Darkweaver cannot reach you."

"But…my mother. No. I'm not staying trapped here and hiding while the one chance to find her passes me by."

Selene stood up. "Mum and Grandma just want Cassie to be safe. I don't care what *you* do."

Julian opened his mouth, his face darkening.

Cassie got to her feet. "Look, I don't want either of you to fight. I can look after myself." She turned to Selene. "We'll stay here tonight, if that's what your mum wants. But we can't just hide, Julian's right. His mother and my parents are missing, and we need to find them. The Cross-Quarter is our chance."

Selene stared at them. "You don't know what he's capable of," she said finally, her voice low and shaking with fierce passion. "He'll kill you both. Like two annoying flies. He doesn't care."

Julian crossed his arms. "There is no need for you or Cassie to put yourselves in danger."

Cassie stared at him. "No way, you're not going anywhere without me!"

He brought the water to his lips, took a sip and swallowed, his Adam's apple moving up and down. A vision swam in Cassie's mind, a scene superimposed upon Julian's body like a film: a parade of young men marching; warriors on their way to battle, and behind them, women; mothers who had nurtured these bodies given up to the world to be slaughtered. Was this real? She blinked and it was gone.

"Let's just rest here for now," said Julian, turning away from them both.

Riveted to the spot by what she had just seen, Cassie said nothing.

"Fine," said Selene. "I am going to tell Grandma you're safe. I suggest you both sleep. It doesn't get dark here. This is all the night you're going to get."

With that, the fox-girl climbed nimbly up the pile of boulders by the entrance, her red hair whipping behind her, and slipped out through the gap in the rocks.

19

*S*elene had been right. The sunset glow of the sky neither deepened nor lightened as they scouted their walled glade for the softest place to rest.

Cassie found a grassy patch between clumps of white flowers by the far wall and sank gratefully to her knees.

"Wonder when she'll be back? Hopefully, no time soon," said Julian, settling cross-legged beside her.

Cassie pressed the palms of her hands into the cool grass. "You don't like her, do you?"

"I don't dislike her."

She tried to ignore the pins and needles in her fingers.

He stretched out, hands clasped behind his head, and closed his eyes. "I don't think she likes *me* much, that's all."

Cassie breathed in and out deeply until the faint, closing-in feeling lessened.

Julian's eyes flashed open. "Are you all right?"

"Yes...I'm okay."

"You look pale."

"Just tired."

He studied her through his eyelashes and then rolled onto his side, propping himself up on one elbow. "That's not why I wanted Selene to stay away, though."

Cassie felt heat rise to her cheeks. "Oh?"

"But we should rest." A tiny smile like a challenge glinted around his eyes.

She eased down beside him and he drew her into the circle of his arms, his heart a drum against her back. Her own heartbeat kicked up, waking her, chasing away the cold, hollow feeling with a fiery warmth.

"I'm not tired now," she whispered.

He didn't move or say anything, and she wondered whether he'd heard. Perhaps he'd fallen asleep. Then, very gently, he removed his arm from beneath her.

"I'm not either."

She rolled over to face him. Her breath caught in her throat at his nearness, the angles of his chin, the smooth plane of his cheeks, the beautiful darkness of his eyes. She touched her mouth to his. Their kiss was careful, gentle. She pressed harder. His breath hitched, and his fingers twined fiercely into her hair. She sailed her palms across his skin beneath his t-shirt. He was a new country, and she was thirsty with novelty, with the wanting of all of him. Gold and red sparked in front of her eyes, patterns of light and swirling dark as she gave herself up to his lips and his hands.

He was strong, stronger than she had ever imagined him to be. There was no trace of the boy in him now. She slid her palms down over his stomach, his hipbones. She wanted to meet this new Julian and know him from the inside out.

A shrill cry came from above.

Julian jolted upright. "What the—?"

The cry came again, its piercing echo bouncing back at them from their rocky fortress.

Cassie saw it first. "There!"

A black eagle several times larger than any eagle she'd seen made a diving swoop above them, sailing over the wall and out of view.

She cast about wildly, searched the towering rock. The eagle called again, but there was no sight of it in the sky. An overhang on the opposite wall caught her eye. She grabbed Julian's hand and sprinted towards it.

"Over here! It won't be able to see us."

They ducked under the ledge together and huddled against the wall.

"I reckon it's already seen us." He shook his head. "We were foolish."

Cassie's throat felt dry as she caught his gaze.

He grasped either side of her face and planted a rough kiss on her lips. "But I don't care."

With her palms against his chest, his warmth blazing up through her arms, she whispered, "Neither do I."

He pulled her against him, and she could feel his heart pounding.

"Cassie!" a voice called from across the clearing.

"It's Selene!" Cassie could make out her slight figure atop the pile of rocks just inside the entrance to their fort.

They watched as she jumped off the rock stack, twirled in the air, and landed as a fox.

Cassie let out a whistle. "She's amazing!"

The next few seconds were a blur as Selene trotted across the glade to join them in their shelter and spun back into a girl before them.

"You've certainly got that down pat," said Julian.

Selene gave him a sharp look, then turned to Cassie. "The Darkweaver knows you're here!"

"You don't say." Julian's snide tone was unsettling, unfamiliar.

Cassie elbowed him, frowning. "Selene, please go on."

"We can't go back, because he'll take the same path we did. The only way is to go forward and hope for a Gate at the other end."

"So you basically led us into a trap."

"Julian!"

Selene turned to him slowly, her green eyes blazing. "How dare you? He was *this close*"—she shoved her thumb and forefinger, with the slightest gap between them in front of his face—"to reaching my home! My mother's home! And *you* are the ones who brought him to us! We were living peacefully before you arrived. So don't tell me I got *you* into this mess."

To Julian's credit, he didn't argue. He even looked slightly ashamed that he'd snapped at her. But Selene hadn't finished with him yet.

"*You're* the liar and concealer! You know you could be so much more help to Cassie, but you haven't got the guts."

Her words made little sense to Cassie, but darkness stretched like an advancing storm across Julian's features and he met Selene's eyes with an expression of such searing hatred that he looked ready to lash out. Instead, he turned his back on them and stalked out of the shelter.

"Julian!" Cassie called.

He broke into a run.

"Come back!"

She leapt out after him, but Selene pulled her back with surprising strength. "It's not safe!"

"But he's...what's he doing?"

Julian was scaling the rock stack up to the entrance to their fortress. Another piercing cry rent the air and a long shadow stretched across him. The next moment was a nightmare. The gigantic eagle swept down and Cassie and Selene watched in horror as it splayed its colossal talons and plucked Julian off the rock, pulling him up and away, his legs kicking and body writhing like a rabbit in the air.

Cassie's scream was louder than the eagle's as she raced out of the shelter, heedless of Selene's calls, stumbling up the rocks after him. But it was no good—within moments, he and the eagle were nothing more than specks above them.

"Julian! Julian!"

Cassie tore her way over the rocks, cutting her hands and knees, shrieking up at the sky until her throat was raw. But there was nothing but the vast, empty firmament above her, as bleak and silver as steel.

She pitched out of the glade and down the other side, racing between the granite tors that were like frozen giants around her, her face wet, her vision blurry. She'd lost the path, but there was nothing within her that cared. She could only run, tripping and sliding down the grassy slope in the direction the bird had flown. If she ran fast enough—

A red blur of fox cut her off, zig-zagging in front of her until she had to stop. She staggered to a standstill, hands on her knees, lungs gasping for air.

"What are you doing?" Selene's voice snapped through her.

"Have to...get him back."

"You mustn't leave the path. You could be trapped here forever."

Cassie shook her head, convulsions of shock and panic wracking through her so that she could hardly breathe.

Selene pulled her by her jumper, directing her to sit on a nearby boulder. Cassie slumped onto the rock, bowing her head, hands over her face, defeat like black swamp water rising to engulf her.

"You want him back?" Selene stood in front of her, arms folded across her chest.

Cassie looked up through her fingers. "Of course I do!"

The fox-girl cocked her head to one side. "Well, you *are* a Spiritweaver."

The pallid, black-eyed face of the Spider Goddess flashed into her mind. She straightened. "You're right!"

She'd changed the Woven once, she could do it again. But *how* had she done it? She grasped the starflower pendant; it felt cold and lifeless. Nothing within her felt calm or in any way magical.

"Do you...did our grandmother tell you anything about how..." She faltered. "Do you know what I should do?"

Selene clambered up next to her. "I don't know, Cassie. Spiritweaver blood doesn't always run true. I can't Weave like Grandma, or your mum. I can only use what they have already woven, like the Gates. Some Walkers can make Gates of their own but I don't know how to."

Cassie kicked the rock with her heel. "If only my mother had taught me something, anything! I don't have a clue how I did it last time."

"Come on then, let's get back on the path and keep going." Selene jumped down. "The bird was heading that way anyway."

Cassie nodded and slid off the rock to join her.

Moving was better than sitting; it did something to quell the panic that was rising like acid within her. Selene took the lead and Cassie settled into a steady stride behind her.

The road wound on through grassland, dotted at first with boulders, then with low shrubs whose leaves, Cassie noticed, were as shiny as mirrors. The wind that she couldn't feel shivered through these plants as it had through the grasses, making their leaves shimmer and shift from dark green to a pale silver where they reflected the sky.

"How long have you been coming to this place?" she asked Selene after a long stretch trudging in silence.

"My whole life."

"So these bubbles are pretty stable then? Like worlds themselves?"

"Yes, but they have boundaries. There are only a few paths you can travel along. And the Gates come and go. Except for Grandma's Gate. That's the one I've always used."

"Who makes the other Gates?"

Selene shrugged as she trotted ahead. "Other Spiritweavers I guess."

"Are there many others that you know of? Who are alive, I mean?"

"No. Only your mum and the Darkweaver, but there might be others."

"What about *your* mother?"

"She can't really do much. A bit with food and herbs, but she couldn't make a Gate or anything."

One of Cassie's feet felt suddenly cold, and she looked down in surprise. She'd taken a step into a shallow puddle. Squelching after Selene, who'd managed a graceful sidestep around the puddle, Cassie noticed that the mirror-leaved shrubs were coalescing, and the grasses receding. As they ventured further on, a few taller shrubs and trees appeared; at first only where trickles of water crossed the track, and then in larger patches until she and Selene were walking through a woodland with bright green ferns and little streams where they had to jump from rock to rock to stay on the track.

Waves of fear continued to surge through Cassie,

followed by the feeling of Julian's hands on her skin, his mouth against hers. By the time they stopped at a larger stream with a bridge across it, her heart was like a burning ball inside her chest and she felt hot and shaky.

"Thirsty?" Selene padded down to the water's edge. "This water's good to drink."

Cassie followed her lead, scooping up handfuls of the clear water. She was indeed thirsty, though she'd not noticed until now. It was sweet and cold and helped to calm the fire within her. Something tugged at her memory, and she paused mid-drink, her cupped handful dripping back into the stream.

"Isn't there some rule about not eating or drinking in—"

"That's only if you're human," cut in Selene, guzzling her water.

"I *am* human!"

Selene gave her an exasperated look. "I mean, if you're not a Walker or a Weaver. A part of you is *of* this land. So of course you won't be harmed by nourishing yourself from it. If you were not, well, that'd be a different story."

"Oh! What about Julian? What if…I just hope he knows that he shouldn't eat or drink anything here."

Selene's lips thinned. "I wouldn't worry about him."

"Why do you dislike him so much? I don't understand. You don't even know him."

The fox-girl caught her gaze with narrowed eyes. "Do you?"

"Do I what?"

"Know him."

Cassie opened her mouth to reply, but the piercing call of the eagle rent the air. Selene hooked Cassie's arm and pulled them both, splashing and slipping, under the bridge.

She needn't have worried about her soaked shoe; now she

was wet up to her knees in icy water. The eagle cried again, and this time it was loud and close.

There was a thud on the bridge above them. They huddled against a pillar of stone felted with moss and algae. Then came a soft thump, and yet another, closer above them, and the wooden slats shook, debris from between the cracks falling into the water below.

Cassie jerked her head down as some of the leaf litter fell into her eyes. Her ankle rolled unevenly on a slippery stone. She stifled a curse and threw her hand out to steady herself against Selene, who caught her, her face white as parchment and her eyes a wide, vivid green. In that moment, she looked so young, surely no more than twelve years old. Cassie pulled her into an unsteady hug. Above the hashing sound of the river, they could hear the scratch of talons as the bird hopped along the bridge towards them. If it bent its head over the edge, it would surely see them and pluck them out with its great beak like whelks from a shell. If she could not save Julian, she would protect her cousin. And she had to do it now. With her resolve, the starflower pendant grew warm against her chest. She gripped it with her left hand and held onto Selene with her right.

"Hold tight," she whispered into the fox-girl's ear.

She concentrated on the water swirling around the rocks at their feet. Its flow was mesmerising. As she watched it, breathing deeply, she felt the starflower grow hot. She need only enter that flow; tweak a little, just like placing a new stone in the swirling water, and the pattern would change. Cassie saw it clearly in her mind's eye, the new path forming, the new circulating flow. With the current thus diverted, she took a step out into the river, pulling Selene along with her.

They were no longer beneath the bridge, but on a patch of bare ground; orange clay scattered with tiny gold stones.

Cassie sat up and a wrenching pain assaulted her, spreading from her chest and burning through her limbs, shooting up her face and over her head. She cried out, but her scream only increased the intensity of the white pain throbbing at her temples.

Cold little hands gripped Cassie's thrashing arms. "It's all right, it's all right. You did it!"

She opened her eyes to Selene crouching beside her with worried eyes. And the pain vanished as abruptly as it had arrived. She sat up, gasping. Selene let her go and kneeled to the ground, her small shoulders rising and falling with quick, shallow breaths. She gave Cassie a cautious smile.

"That was definitely stranger than a Change."

Cassie let out a strangled sound that was something between a laugh and a sob, her head giddy with relief. "Where are we?"

"I don't know, I've never been here."

They took in their surroundings. The patch of bare ground looked to be a clearing in a dense forest. The contrast between the light, open ground and the dark forest around them was so great that it felt as though a giant spotlight had been turned upon them. It was hard to see very far in front of them, and impossible to make out anything amongst the surrounding trees.

They helped each other to their feet and in unspoken agreement, headed for the forest edge. Cassie felt a sudden sympathy with the chooks her dad had once kept, and their constant eyeing of the sky with concerned, beady eyes.

They made it across the clearing and slid gratefully under the shelter of the trees. There was no sign of a track, and a stream barred their way.

"We could find a way across, I suppose," said Cassie, scouting for a log or rocks that they could use.

"Yes, but we still don't know where the path is. I say we follow the stream."

"I say you don't," came a voice from behind them.

They whirled around. At the edge of the forest, with the light of the clearing like a halo behind him, stood Dominic.

20

"*D*arkweaver!" hissed Selene, spinning into a snarling fox before Cassie had even made sense of who had appeared there.

"Oh, lovely. My two nieces come to play."

Cassie clenched her jaw. "You are not family."

The Darkweaver laughed. "We've been through this, my dear. Now come with me, I want to show you something."

He turned his back on them, and Selene, snapping and growling, leapt at him and sank her teeth into his calf. He spun with quicksilver speed, flinging her off him. She landed splayed on the ground, sprang back to her feet and leapt at him again, yowling. This time he kicked out, landing an audible blow against her side. She fell, whimpering, to the forest floor. He advanced on her and pulled his foot back for a second blow.

Cassie screamed and dived to cover Selene with her own body. The kick connected with Cassie's ribs. She gasped and curled over the still body of her cousin.

"Get up," ordered the Darkweaver.

Cassie buried her face into Selene's fur. With relief, she realised she could hear Selene's quick-racing heart.

"Get up!"

Dominic yanked Cassie's arm and pulled her from Selene with such strength that she felt like a rag doll. His impassive face gleamed, white and angled, in the half-light of the forest as he looked down at Selene's unmoving form.

"Filthy creature."

He pulled Cassie through a tangle of vegetation to the edge of the clearing and shoved her ahead of him into the light, keeping a firm hold of her arm.

"Walk."

He marched her to the centre of the clearing and spun her around so that she was facing away from the forest. Then, with a lazy wave of his fingers, an invisible veil lifted, revealing three huge, transparent orbs hovering above the orange earth, oscillating at the edges like enormous drops of water. Floating within each orb, eyes closed as though sleeping, were people wearing red scarves. Cassie took in their faces in disbelief: Ben, Lyra, Violeta.

She blinked and stared, trying to make sense of what she was seeing. Then her chest tightened. Those were not scarves. She reeled, and the Darkweaver held her like a vice. It was blood. All of it. A frozen stream issuing from a red gash at each throat.

Her knees buckled and all the breath left her body, but Dominic tightened his grip and grasped her chin and held her so that she couldn't look away from the scene before her.

"They're not dead. Not yet."

She could move only her eyes to look at him. His face was alight, gleeful. "How—"

"You ask me how? Not why?" He loosened his grip.

185

"That's my girl. A Darkweaver at heart. I tried to tell you. But showing you is so much better."

He tilted his head to the side as though joining her in the examination of an intriguing art installation.

"I don't need you, you know. In all honesty, I was beginning to think you were just like my mother, just like my sister. But there is potential in you. I would like us to learn to work together. You see? That's all."

Cassie forced herself to look at him. "And you think that by hurting everyone I love, I'll choose you?"

Dominic laughed and Cassie cursed the bell-like sound of it, the way it brought the sunlight dancing all around them.

"It's not a question of choice, Cassie. Do you see the beautiful one there—Violeta? I tried to cure her of her beastliness, to purify her. She also thought I was giving her a choice. No, I am the only one who gets to choose, I'm afraid."

Her mother, her father, their blood, was all Cassie could see. And Violeta. Longed for, grieved for Violeta. Here she was, her dark hair fanned out behind her as though she had dived into a pool, her arms flung wide, fingers curled in, eyes closed and face as pale as Cassie had ever seen it. Julian, you were right. Julian.

She couldn't comprehend the sight of her father. His solid warmth, his easy smile, the way he cared for her, tending to her with the same patience he showed his garden; allowing her unfolding, making trellises for her wildness—none of that was here now. His sun-browned skin was grey. It couldn't be him. Her father lived in sunshine and peace. Not here. Not like this.

And Lyra. She couldn't even look at her. Her heart would burst. To have missed her mother, her own true home, and to have finally found her. No. It could not be.

Black despair welled up within her. Her muscles slackened, and she fell to her knees, bowing her head, her fingers clutching into the pebbles and dust. The starflower swung out in front of her, dull and lifeless.

"What you get," she heard the Darkweaver crunching on the gravel to her right as he paced out long strides back and forth beside her, "is this: not a choice, rather an offer." He stopped pacing. "Come home with me and I let two of these souls free. You get to decide which two. The other will die. You can think of it as my commission. Or perhaps as a little reminder, in case you ever forget who is the stronger of the two of us. Because I intend to train you, Cassie, to bequeath you with my knowledge. I need someone to take on the business when I am gone, as I've not yet discovered how to cheat death and my son is a powerless lump. And who better than family to continue the family business?"

She stared up at him uncomprehendingly. "You have a son?"

"Oh *do* get up, Cassie. I'll strain my neck looking down at you there in the dirt."

Cassie didn't move. He hauled her to her feet, and holding her arm in an iron grip, pulled her around to face him, close enough that she could smell the tang of aniseed on his breath.

"What do you say, my dear?"

Cassie said nothing.

He slapped her.

She gasped, bringing her hand to her burning cheek.

"You say: *Thank you uncle, for your kind regard.*"

The slap woke something within Cassie, as though the molten mess of her despair had been plunged into icy water and made into something strong and sharp, tempered into steel. She kept her head bowed as the fierce strength of her rage coursed around her body and into the starflower until it burned against her skin.

Then she saw it: how she could un-weave him. It was before her in the space of all that could be, in the screen of her mind, laid out like burning thread through a labyrinth, and all she had to do was follow it to its centre. She found the end of the flaming thread. She need only twist and pull. She raised her chin.

Dominic's eyes widened, and for a moment she saw a flash of fear across his features, then the thread was pulled from the grasp of her mind and dashed into darkness. Dominic reared up in front of her, a vicious fountain of rage.

"How dare you!"

He swiped downwards, and she felt a burning slice across her back as she fell to the ground, all the breath forced from her lungs. She sat up, gasping, and another slice like a whip struck her again.

"You have no idea what you are doing. You ignorant, foolish child!"

He kicked her, the point of his boot striking her in the ribs, and despite herself, she cried out. Then he squatted beside her and yanked her by the hair, hissing into her ear. "Try that again and you will join your parents. I am out of patience. That was your last chance. Submit, Cassie. You are done."

The sky darkened above them. Dominic glanced up and quickly got to his feet as an eagle the size of a small plane landed in the clearing. The Darkweaver strode towards it.

"Where's the boy?"

The eagle lifted its wings and shuffled its feathers in a disgruntled fashion.

The Darkweaver took a square silver object from his jacket pocket and pointed it at the bird, which immediately began to revolve in front of them, its body shrinking and feathers receding until it became a man, stumbling for balance. He was slight, with a greyish, hawklike face, and he wore a crumpled blue suit, ripped at the front and dark with something that looked like blood.

"Cassie, meet Mercer. Mercer, this is my niece. She is your better, remember that. Unfortunately, she requires some discipline, which I need you to enforce. Restrain her while I question you."

Dominic had regained his composure, though Cassie could feel the dangerous undercurrent beneath the velvet of his voice. As Mercer made his way towards her, she hauled herself to her feet. Bruises were swelling at her ribs and on her cut-up knees and she could feel the burning of welts across her back. But she wouldn't give the Darkweaver the satisfaction of knowing how much pain she was in. She would stand upright before them both. Mercer was not as slight up close, and stronger even, than Dominic. Without hesitation or expression on his pinched face, he grasped her arms and twisted them up behind her back.

"Good. Now take the necklace from her and give it to me."

Cassie started and struggled, but Mercer's hold on her was firm as he reached out to grasp the starflower pendant. As soon as his palm touched it, though, a spark flashed from it. Mercer cried out and snatched his hand away.

Only a tightening around the eyes betrayed any senti-ment from Dominic. "No matter. Cassie will be gifting me with it soon enough. Now, Mercer, where is the boy?"

"He bit me. Made me drop him." Mercer sounded sullen.

"*Bit* you?" Dominic rubbed a hand across his forehead. "Have you no respect for Thorne's memory? For your better? It was to be a life for a life, Mercer." He made a disgusted sound. "You're all the same. A disgrace and a waste of space."

Mercer said nothing, but gave Cassie's arms a painful shove. She gasped and blinked her watering eyes, which drew Dominic's gaze to her face.

"Well, Cassie? Who gets to stay? Who gets to go? It's time for you to decide."

"I will do no such thing," Cassie ground out the words.

The Darkweaver took a step towards her. "You won't choose?"

"I will not."

"Then all three shall perish, I'm afraid. As you wish. I tire of this game anyway."

He swivelled around to face the orbs and raised his arms.

"Wait!"

There was a vicious smile on his face as he turned back to her. "Changed your mind?"

"Why?"

He cocked his head to one side. "Why what, sweet niece?"

"Why...all this?"

Dominic's lips curled. "I see you have little appreciation for the Arts. We shall be able to rectify that over time, I'm sure." He took a step towards her. "Can you not see the beauty in it? Look at them."

Cassie locked eyes with him and did not budge.

"Mercer, make her look."

Mercer's thumb and forefinger dug into her cheeks and turned her face to her parents and Violeta, suspended and motionless within their watery prisons.

"There. You see? Aren't they exquisite?"

All Cassie could think of was to keep him talking. She began to shiver, and cursed her body for betraying her. *The boy*. Julian. It must be him. He must be alive. The alternative wasn't something she could entertain.

"What's his name?"

"Who's name?"

"Your son's."

Dominic narrowed his eyes. "My son," he sneered, "is a worthless piece of lard and not worth a moment of your thought."

Cassie tried to lift her chin within Mercer's grip. "Still, as he's my cousin, shouldn't I at least know his name?"

The Darkweaver sniffed. "His name is Elias."

"May I meet him?"

"No, you may not. Now—"

"Julian," she said quickly. "His mother, Violeta. Why her?"

"Well, aren't we full of questions? Mercer, turn her around."

The Walker released his grip on her face and hauled her about on the spot. Dominic stepped up close behind her. The trembling in her jaw made her teeth click together in the silence. She flinched as he swept the curtain of her hair over her shoulder and ran his hand down the bare skin of her neck. Her shivering must have been visible to him, and she wished she could stop. She felt him clasp his fingers around her hands, drawing them downwards, releasing her from Mercer's hold, and then a cord snaked around her wrists, binding them tightly.

"You may go now, Mercer. Find the boy. If he's alive, bring him to me."

Mercer turned for the centre of the clearing. Dominic drew out the silver box again and pointed it towards him. "Oh and tell him I have his sweetheart. That might encourage him to come without a fight."

The Darkweaver pressed a button on the silver box, and

191

Mercer turned from man to bird, leaping up and out of the clearing with heavy wingbeats.

"There, that's better. His stench was gumming up my nostrils."

He sighed and looked down at her with the air of a dancer in his final pose of a routine, and Cassie had the absurd notion he expected applause. Then, like a snake, he snatched her, pinned her tightly with his arms and legs and whispered into her ear, his breath hot against her cheek. "Do you want to know about Violeta?"

Cassie froze.

He let out a disdainful snort and released her with a jerk. "Of course you do."

With a leering, mocking bow, he stepped back from her and began to pace, his long jacket swishing in dramatic twirls behind him.

"She was sweet. As fine a woman as a man could hope to know."

Nausea rose in Cassie's stomach. "How did you know her?"

Dominic paused and raised his eyebrows. "You cannot guess?"

Cassie breathed shallowly and shook her head. The Dark-weaver resumed his pacing.

"It was in searching for you, actually, that I came across the enchanting Violeta Walcott. Your mother hid you well. For years, I didn't know I had a niece. Your mother...well, for a long time I made it my business to keep as far from her as possible, not knowing, you see, whether she sought retribution. For our own dear mother, that is. I can't say I wanted to find out particularly. But when your aunt Maree let slip one day that our sister had a child...well, it tickled me to find out more about you. To see where your strengths lay, so to speak."

He stopped pacing and eyed her in an abruptly canny, reptilian way. She flinched, and his lips curled into a slow smile before turning his back on her for another round of pacing.

"It wasn't too hard to find you after that, to set old Thorne up to watch you all and give me news of you. But then Thorne got wind of your unusual neighbours. I'd wondered what had drawn my sister to live out near the old Curwood. And Thorne gave me the answer. He brought Violeta to me. He knew I'd find her useful. But"—he sighed again—"I did not count on feeling anything for her. I have never in all my life wanted to purify a Walker so much as I wanted to her." Dominic's eyes grew bright. "I set to work trying, not just to control the affliction, as I have with Mercer, but to cure her."

Cassie shook her head. "What do you mean?"

He frowned. "What do I mean?"

"Is Violeta a...Spiritwalker?"

Dominic's eyes widened, and then his face broke into a mask of glee. "You truly didn't know?"

He began to laugh, and the glade rained with golden fire. He laughed and laughed until all Cassie could hear was the ringing of his voice in her head and all she could see was blinding light.

"Oh, this is good, too good," she heard him say as finally, Cassie's legs gave way beneath her.

She curled up on the ground where she fell, clenching her eyes shut. Violeta. A Walker. Like Selene. Had her mother known? Known all this? Had her father? One hundred days of childhood flashed through her mind. Her mother carrying her through the forest, singing to her at bedtime; her father guiding her hands in the soil to bury tiny seeds; their hands, their smiles, their laughter. Was all of it layered upon lies? And Violeta. Her kind eyes and lilting voice, her stories and her food. Was any of it real? And Julian? She shivered. What about Julian?

The smell of aniseed hit her like a wall, and she opened her eyes with a start. Dominic was squatting beside her, peering into her face. She scrambled to sit, to push herself away from him. He grasped her hand.

"Dear Cassie. Your world is crumbling. All the people you loved have lied to you. I have not lied. Not one word I have said to you is an untruth." He pulled her to him, and she didn't struggle as he cradled her against his chest. "Let me teach you. Show you the ways. We are here to control those of beastly nature. To prevent them from wreaking havoc on the unknowing world of ordinary people. That's not such a terrible thing, is it? You could do good, Cassie."

His words were like a quietly flowing river, crooning and caressing. She closed her eyes. "And I promise," he said as he stroked her hair, "that I will never lie to you."

21

*J*ulian cursed himself as he pushed through the tangle of shrubs. Their mirror-like leaves sent blinding flashes into his eyes as he parted them, serving only to disorient him further. The gashes below his shoulders where the bird's talons had ripped through into muscle were throbbing, and he was aware of a wet sensation seeping down his chest and back. The heat of his wounds and the cold, draining feeling of his emptying blood were a dizzying combination, but he stumbled forward, knowing that he must find Cassie.

The eagle had kept the track beneath them for much of their flight, but it was only once they'd entered the forest and it had flown low beneath the trees that Julian had taken his chance. The Change had been especially painful in the eagle's grip, but he'd managed to twist around and bite down hard on its talons. It had let him go with a shriek and he had fallen, tumbling over and over in the air. He must have blacked out on impact, because he remembered nothing but waking in human form with a web of branches above him and a stabbing pain at the back of his head.

Cassie. How could he have left her? This was punishment for his blind rage. Selene was not, and never had been, the cause of his anger; he knew that now. His rage was directed at himself, at the truth that Selene had only spoken aloud. It was true, he could have been so much more use to Cassie if only he'd not been so cowardly, if only he hadn't valued her love and regard more than the help he could have provided her as a beast. It was a choice between the two. Once she knew him for what he was, she would feel the full weight of his betrayal, his years of hiding from her. And—he allowed himself to see this fully now—she could not love him. The way his father could not love his mother. Of that, he was sure.

With a splash, he staggered out onto a path dotted with silver puddles. There were footprints in the mud between them. Two sets. One smaller than the other. His heart kicked inside his ribs. Cassie and Selene. It had to be them. He tried to ignore the growing dizziness and picked up his pace. But it grew harder and harder to see through blurred vision and eyes that wanted to close. With a groan, he fell to the ground. The only way forward was to Change. He had more stamina as a beast; perhaps it would take him as far as he needed to go. He curled into a ball. If he could manage it. The green woods and grey sky shifted and tilted in front of his eyes. He must do it now. Before he slipped away into darkness. He writhed, reaching for the body of the beast, feeling for the tide to take him.

The next he knew was a duller pain, but a keener sense of his lifeblood, reeking of salt and iron, trickling down his paws into the mud. With a snarl, he slunk forwards, nose pointed along the path upon their trail.

He sniffed the air and the track for traces of girl or fox. Cassie's trail was as ephemeral as the scent of violets, intoxicating one moment and gone the next, a fleeting, enigmatic thing. Selene's was the more reliable of the two, and he followed it with unwavering discipline, hoping against hope that they had not been parted.

As he approached a bridge, the smell of eagle joined the two. His stomach churned. He traced the girls to the water's edge and saw their tracks in the mud. They had hidden beneath this bridge. From the eagle? He ran back and forth across the bridge with an increasing sense of despair on each pass, as he found no sign that they had reached the other side to continue their journey. The trail ended abruptly beneath the bridge. That much was clear. This, combined with the evidence that the eagle was here, could lead him to only one conclusion.

With a howl, he raced across the bridge and away from the sound of the water, deeper into the forest. There was nothing to do but follow this path, follow it to the end, and hope that he might find them there.

An hour or so later, with the sun lighting golden pathways through the forest in its eternal sunset, Julian began to wish he'd taken some water from the river to drink. Although the bleeding had lessened, the throbbing ache from the region of his wounds had grown, and the path ahead was blurring. He wove back and forth across the track until he staggered to a standstill and, despite his desperation to continue, found his body failing him as he collapsed to the ground.

There was no sound, not a stirring of leaf or the cracking of a twig. Or was it that he could no longer hear the world? The light was fading after all, from gold to deepest night. He no longer felt cold or weary, and the pain seemed a far-away thing, a mere colour, a red flicker in the darkness.

A spark the colour of fox. And there, a sliver of green; the forest in spring flush. Hands at his face, the softest voice urging him to drink. Cold wetness against his tongue. Now someone grooming his fur, nudging him. Curling up against him and lending him their warmth.

~

CASSIE LAY STILL as a rock in a river. The Darkweaver's hands glided down her hair, her back, around her waist and up to the starflower, resting cold against her breastbone. Her eyes were squeezed shut, but she could hear his breath; short and ragged in her ear. She was no longer trembling. Every nerve ending was screaming at her to move, to kick, to writhe, but she could not.

He exhaled, and his whispering voice was thick with pleasure. "Your gift to me."

Any small hope that the pendant would spark as it had done with the eagle Walker faded as he grasped and tugged at the starflower. The chain cut into the back of her neck, but the catch did not release. Dominic lifted the pendant, but as he tried to pull it over her head, the chain grew smaller and smaller until it sat like a choker above her collarbone. He reached up to unclasp it, fiddling and pulling, but it would not open. He shoved her back and stood up.

"I can see I'll have to remove your pretty head to receive my gift."

Blessedly released from her frozen state, Cassie scrambled to her feet and staggered from him. He closed the gap with a few elegant strides and gripped her by the arm.

"Come now, we haven't finished our game. I told you

about Violeta, who would leave me rather than allow herself to be purified and stand at my side. Now you must decide her fate. You may think you love your parents, Cassie, but these three are liars and they must meet their judgement. Choose now. Who will be spared by your mercy, and who shall pay for their crimes?"

She stared at the ground, willing herself to remain standing, to think of something, anything, that could stall him.

"You said...you wanted to...purify Violeta." She tilted her head away from Dominic's. "Why do you want to hurt her now?"

The Darkweaver's fingernails dug into Cassie's arm and for several moments she could hear only his breath. Then he exhaled shortly through his nose, an amused sound, and hissed into her hair. "Apparently, I was not to her taste. I would never dream of forcing such a woman."

Cassie couldn't help herself. "No, you *murder* her instead!"

"Cassie, her life is in *your* hands. Not mine."

"I want them all released."

"That is not the deal."

Cassie felt hot anger washing through her finally, burning away the numbness and terror. "A deal is where both parties stand to gain something!"

She struggled, kicking out at his shins.

"How delightful. What a wildcat you are!"

"Let me go!"

He wrapped a leg around her kicking one, pinning her in a grip again like a python. "One death for your life and two of theirs. I would say you are getting the better part of the bargain."

She stopped struggling. "Then take my life and set them all free."

He laughed. "Goodness no! A saintly offer, but not one I'm willing to accept. You need only take one life. One."

"I will not."

He spun her around, and she was surprised to see the amusement in his face replaced by frustration.

"I'm doing this for you. Choose, and then you can truly become my apprentice. I saw it in you, niece. That first moment in my offices when you drew my energy into yourself with such unconscious ease. I've never seen anything like it. Even I could not do that without training. Even I. You have more lying latent within you than you know. You are a Darkweaver. Can't you see that it's what you already are? I can help you. No one else has cared enough to train you, to show you how to use what is rightfully yours. One life, and you can become like me."

Cassie stared.

"I will ask no more death of you after this. You can use your talent as you will. But it isn't right for you not to know. Believe me, I know what it's like to have the power but not the knowledge. I won't let that happen to you."

"Yet only a moment ago you wanted to remove my head," she said evenly.

"I was frustrated, Cassie. I get that way. Many years of being alone, having whatever it is I desire with no need to ask for it has made me an impatient man. You can keep the pendant. I won't try to take it from you again."

Cassie made no move, her mind reeling.

"Will you do this, niece? If not for me, then for yourself. One sacrifice for a life of freedom. Freedom to do much good in the world if that is what you choose. Darkweaving is not inherently bad. It is merely a mode, a technology. Like the type of energy you choose to power your house. You may use it in any way you'd like."

Cassie began to shiver again. "Then why the sacrifice?"

"It seems the lessons begin," said Dominic, stepping back a pace and meeting her gaze, all traces of humour gone from his handsome features. "Because there is a Power who requires it. She of many names. The oldest Weaver of all."

Cassie breathed in sharply. "The Spider Goddess."

"You know of her?" Dominic raised his brows.

"She came to...visit me. After I...after I left you."

"And yet you stand before me unharmed." He stared at her. "Still more proof of your capacity. There are few who have looked upon her face and remain to tell the tale."

"She warned me. Against being reckless with the Woven."

"Then I think you will not receive many more warnings from her. She is not known for her clemency."

"How do you do it then? Get away with so much?"

He smiled again, a smile that did not quite reach his eyes. "I give her what she requires, when she requires it. And she leaves me be."

A cold spark arced down Cassie's spine.

"And what she requires of you now, Cassie, is a life."

A howl, followed by a guttural growl and a blur of black and red, filled the space between them. For a moment, there was only chaos. Dominic's scream and an inhuman snarling sound resounded through the clearing. Cassie, her arms still bound behind her, stood rooted to the spot with fear, until it became clear that the attack—for that was what it appeared to be—was directed solely at the Darkweaver. In the tumbling mass of fur and claws and teeth before her, she thought she could make out Selene, as well as another, larger, darker shape. She shivered with relief and fear. Selene had survived. She thought of the petrified tree beings they'd encountered along the way here. Selene had friends in this world—of course! And she had clearly rallied one or more of them to help her.

The fight did not last long. Within moments, Selene was lying immobile at Cassie's feet, tossed away with a cry of rage by the Darkweaver. Cassie fell to her knees and leaned over her cousin.

"Selene, can you hear me?"

The fox-girl whimpered, and Cassie saw that her tiny chest was rising and falling unevenly and that there were frothing red bubbles at her snout. Her strangely delicate mouth fell open to reveal white canines and the black line of her gum.

"Selene, stay with me, please stay with me." She leaned over the fox, her hair curtaining them both. For a moment, she heard only her cousin's rasping breath.

The next sound was a sickening thud as the second creature was thrown to the ground by the Darkweaver. Cassie squeezed her eyes shut.

"Open your eyes!"

The rageful triumph of Dominic's voice extinguished the tiny flame of hope that had dared to blossom in her chest.

"Look at the vile beast before me. See how it has fallen. Now you understand why we must rule them, contain and control them."

She turned her gaze unwillingly to the man towering before her; his eyes were feverish, his face torn by claw-marks and his hands red with blood.

"Look!"

At Dominic's feet, lying on its side, was a huge black dog. Cassie shivered. Seeping patches of blood were already turning the orange gravel beneath it black. The Darkweaver kicked the dog, and it gave a weak yelp.

He dug the silver box out from within his jacket, aimed it at the dog as though it were a gun, and pressed the button.

"The last lie, Cassie."

He hurled the box at the dog and it connected with its flank with a nauseating crack. Then he spat on the ground, turned his back on the beast and strode to where Cassie stood, aghast. The dog writhed and stretched before her eyes, its fur receding, hind-limbs lengthening, all in a whirling blur, until lying on his side, brown arms and bloody t-shirt, his dark hair falling across one cheek, lay Julian Walcott.

Cassie gasped. The earth would not be still beneath her. The world was closing in around her. Julian. A Walker. Julian. Her ears were ringing, and her hands felt cold. It could not be. Yet hadn't a part of her always known? The dogs in the forest, at her house. The one she'd followed to safety in the dark. Now it all made sense. A terrible sense. The last lie indeed. The blackness closed in, and all the world was gone.

SHE OPENED her eyes with a start to the Darkweaver's face above hers.

"Wake up, wake up!"

His triumphant expression chilled her to her core. There, on the ground before them, lay the still forms of Selene—no longer a fox, but a slight, wan figure, lying on a pillow of her red hair—and Julian, his eyes closed. She struggled towards them, but the Darkweaver clamped hold of her arm.

"Let the fallen be! Come. In this dark hour when the veil between worlds is thinnest, it is time to make your choice."

Veil between worlds? The Cross-Quarter. Had the night

turned to day already, unknown to Cassie in this land where the sun never set? Her heart screamed at her and she closed her eyes to a swimming vision of Alisa in the library, a time that seemed aeons ago now.

For tonight is Halloween, when the fairy folk ride. And they that would let true love win, at Miles Cross must bide.

Or something like that. Poor Alisa. So many years of searching for her lost love. Believing ancient rhymes from a far-off country. When the truth was so much darker than the simple ballad would have it. So much more a thing of earth and stone and blood. Here, now, the only loves Cassie had ever known were strewn about her in this glade, their lifeblood flowing from them, and she, unable to help any of them. There would be no saving them with romantic rhymes or heroic deeds. She was no heroine. Bloody and sore and weak, the fight within her was gone. She would turn to the Darkweaver, tell him a name, and then she would die, because no one could make such a choice and live.

She clasped the starflower. It was warm, like a quietly living thing. But it gave her no hope. Her uncle would thwart any shift she tried to make in the Woven. The face of the Spider Goddess floated in her mind. Eyes like coal. Lips, wet and red. Pale cheeks pinked with anticipation. Was it a vision? Or was it her that Cassie could see out of the corner of her eye, waiting?

She tore her gaze from Julian and took a step towards the glowing orbs, aware of the Darkweaver's gaze on her. She took in each of their faces.

"I love you," she whispered to them.

And then she turned to the Darkweaver.

"Your choice?"

"I choose..."

A thought occurred to her. A reckless gambit. But surely

that black, hulking thing—dark furred spindles holding up a squatting mass at the edge of her vision—was no mere shadow. It was truly her. Ready to seize her prey. Awaiting only Cassie's decision. And Cassie had nothing left to lose.

"I choose...I choose you, Dominic Darkweaver. You will be the sacrifice for my Lady of Many Names!"

It happened in an instant. A vortex like a black hole took up Cassie's entire field of vision and within it she saw the Spider Goddess snatch and hold Dominic's struggling body within a pair of her black-clawed legs, and his face was wild with shock and fear.

Thank you, Spiritweaver. A rich gift indeed. This morsel has long altered the Woven for his own designs. On occasion, it has amused me. But I find I tire of the labour of reweaving in his wake. You have saved me much effort. Be sure you do not repeat his mistakes.

Her black eyes trained themselves on Dominic and she bent towards him, placing her dark lips against his. He slackened as the Spider Goddess kissed him, and her body turned from black to a gold so bright that Cassie had to close her eyes. When she opened them again, both Dominic and the Spider Goddess had gone, leaving only a dark spiral that receded into a black dot and then vanished.

22

*C*assie's hands were no longer bound. The orbs had also disappeared. On the ground below the place each silvery prison had hovered, lay three prostrate figures. Cassie ran to them, a sudden fear churning within her that in doing away with the Darkweaver, she had killed them all.

Her fears were allayed as soon as she reached them. Lyra was the first to sit up, with a dazed expression, but with no sign of blood or wound anywhere upon her.

"Mum!" Cassie threw herself at her.

"Oh! My darling girl!"

She was home. A Cassie in a Lyra tree, within her mother's arms, a place she'd never thought she'd be again. And yet, her mother's frame seemed smaller than she remembered, Cassie's arms as strong as Lyra's in the force of their embrace. And as they drew back to gaze at one another, Cassie saw her own eyes looking back at her, worried, loving and full of unshared secrets.

"I'm sorry, Cassie, I'm so sorry." Lyra pulled her again

into a hug, and they rocked together there until Cassie did not know who was comforting whom.

Another pair of arms came around them both then and Cassie knew him without opening her eyes. She would always know him from all others by the way he smelt of sunshine, if sunshine had a scent of its own. Her parents were alive, and for a moment, the world was right again.

And then the moment passed. Through a gap beneath Ben's arms, she could see Violeta, bowed over Julian's still form.

"Violeta."

They released each other and Cassie stumbled across the gravel to Violeta's side, where she kneeled with a hand on Julian's chest. She glanced up at Cassie, her beautiful eyes wide in her drawn face.

"*Mi hijo*. He breathes."

Cassie kneeled beside her and placed her own hand over Violeta's.

"He does."

Ben called from Selene's side. "She's alive."

"We have to get them home," said Lyra, joining them beside Julian. "But first, Cassie, hold your pendant and give me your other hand."

Cassie did as her mother directed, and Lyra placed a palm over the wound at Julian's shoulder. The starflower began to warm until it was as hot as a brick after a day in the sun. Then she felt a pleasant tingling flow from hand to pendant, through her chest, her other arm, and down into her mother's hand. Cassie couldn't see the wound beneath Lyra's fingers, but after several minutes, Julian awoke with a gasp. He tried to sit up, but Violeta placed a hand against his cheek.

"Hush, *mi hijo querido*."

Julian's eyes widened. "Mamá? Am I dead?"

Violeta broke into one of her wide smiles Cassie remembered so well. "No, my love, we are alive."

Julian's gaze wandered across them all in astonishment, pausing at Cassie before glancing away.

A great cry rent the air and a shadow fell over them. An eagle swooped low, landing in the clearing with a skid and a hop.

"Mercer!" Cassie scrambled to her feet. The others looked up, startled. "The box!"

She spotted its glint of silver by Julian's foot and ran to pick it up. It was flat and smooth, and weighed less than a phone in her hands. It had one slightly raised button, and nothing else that she could see. She aimed it directly at the eagle, hoping she was pointing it the right way. A tingling sensation with something of the starflower pendant's warmth played around her fingers as she pressed the button, and the eagle revolved rapidly into a man on his hands and knees. He staggered upright, lurching as he ran at Cassie, his face twisted in anger.

But Mercer's blows never fell on Cassie; a crowd of bodies brought him down: Ben, Julian, Violeta and Lyra all falling upon him. Lyra cupped her hands to her mouth, whispering and releasing invisible words into the air as though they were butterflies. Seconds later, a slithering, rasping sound filled the glade. Green vines invaded the clearing, snaking in from the forest edge, heading with startling singularity for Mercer. Cassie and the others leapt back and within moments, the leafy ropes had him pinned to the ground.

Cassie stared at her mother, who gave her a bashful smile.

"You are *so* going to have to teach me how to do that."

Lyra's expression was suddenly solemn. "I promise you. I

will. No more secrets between us."

Cassie turned to the eagle Walker. "Dominic is gone. I don't know what was between you. But you are no longer his slave, or employee, or whatever. If you promise to let us be, we'll let you go."

Mercer met her eyes with a long, hard stare. Then he swallowed. "Gone?"

Cassie met his stare. "Forever."

His eyes flickered to the others standing above him, and she saw a subtle shift in his jaw. Then he gave a curt nod.

Cassie stepped back. "Mum?"

Lyra's eyes narrowed at Mercer. "A promise?"

"I promise to do no harm to any of you."

Lyra lifted her arm, and the vines slithered back from Mercer. He got warily to his feet.

"I'll need that," he said, motioning to the silver box in Cassie's hands.

"Why?"

"He made it so I can't Change without it."

"He *what*?" It was Julian, speaking for the first time, a horrified expression on his face.

"'That's how he made us his to command."

Violeta stepped forward and took Mercer's hand swiftly into her own. He looked as shocked as Cassie felt. "You are free now. No one can control you anymore. Your life is your own. Cassie? What do you say?"

Cassie looked from Violeta and Mercer to her mother. "What do you think?"

Lyra met her eyes with a wistful expression. "I think you've been making some very good decisions without my help. I trust you on this one."

Cassie took a breath. "All right Mercer. You can keep this. But I want you to do something for me. I want you to find my cousin, Elias, and tell him of his father's death. I believe he would be the owner of Drake Industries now. Unless you know more than I do?"

Mercer cast his eyes to the ground. "You are right. I will let him know. And then I will leave him to it."

Cassie nodded and passed him the silver box. "Good for you."

They held their breath as Mercer walked from them into the centre of the clearing. He placed the box in his mouth and within seconds was swirling and shifting into a large black eagle, the device held neatly in his beak. With a deep flap, he took off and soared up over the forest canopy and away.

With Selene still unconscious, there was no possibility of walking back to the Weaver Gate through which they'd entered, so Lyra removed herself from the others in an attempt (her first, apparently) to create a new Gate home.

Julian stood quietly by his mother. Cassie sat pillowing Selene in her lap while Dad explained to her in hushed tones how Dominic had made a Gate directly into their home. He had seen Lyra and Violeta in their horrific watery cells for only moments, and then he knew nothing else.

He had his arm around her shoulder, pulling her into his warmth; and for a moment she felt peace. She glanced up. Julian would not meet her eye.

Two black dogs dancing in a clearing. The memory of their howls still sent shivers up her spine. Yet here they were: the two people she cherished the most outside of her family. And she realised she'd known even then as she'd watched them in that golden light that she loved them, and that some-how, they were known to her.

She opened her mouth to speak, to call Julian to her side, to tell him it was all right, that nothing need change, that it was only truth, and that it could never hurt them, but Lyra gave a yell of triumph and they all turned to see. Her mother had conjured a glowing auric square in the centre of the clearing.

"Quick, let's go through while it holds!"

Ben scooped Selene into his arms, and one by one they stepped through; the now-familiar tugging and twisting as nauseating as ever to Cassie as she landed with a thump on the lawn at the back of their house on Pardalote Lane. Lyra was the last to appear, releasing the square of light like a curtain behind her.

"Mum, that was brilliant!"

"Let's get her inside," said Lyra, rushing forward to help Ben with Selene, but she shot a small, pleased smile at Cassie as she brought Selene's arm across her shoulders.

VIOLETA AND JULIAN took their leave not long after arriving home.

"Will you return to the big house?" Cassie asked her.

"No. No, John Walcott's house is no longer my home."

"Stay here with us then," Lyra urged.

But Violeta shook her head and linked her arm with Julian's.

"I have a place for us to go. We will be well. I'll come and visit soon. Julian too, I'm sure. His father will be missing him." She smiled at her son. "For now, we all need to rest."

They left in a flurry of rattling autumn wind that whirled the leaves into eddies at everyone's feet. Cassie watched Julian follow his mother out across the lawn. *Turn around Julian. Look at me. Say goodbye.* But he didn't. And by the time Cassie thought to call out or follow, they had already gone.

23

*A*li and Maree's arrival helped a little to fill the absence left by Julian and Violeta. Maree fussed over a recovering Selene in a way Cassie could not have imagined Selene tolerating. Indeed, after several days of it, Cassie began to detect a fair degree of irritation mixed in with the affection the wildly independent fox-girl showed for her mother.

On one foggy morning, Ali and Cassie walked together in the garden. The last of the borage flowers and bright orange splashes of calendulas glowed in the mist amongst the young tendrils of snow peas along the fence.

"Were you sad to have missed the Cross-Quarter?"

Cassie had been wanting to venture this question since Ali had first arrived, but they'd had little time alone together.

Ali drew a long breath. "Yes." She stopped walking and turned to face Cassie. "But I was more upset to have lost you and Julian. If I hadn't gone to see Nellie...I wanted to know...well, it doesn't matter now. Not for another year. I'm just so sorry I left you alone."

Cassie met Ali's worried gaze. "I'm glad you weren't there. He was...he would have hurt you too. He hurt everyone I loved."

"And everyone you loved has hurt you."

Cassie started. "No, that's not true."

"Yes. We all lied to you in one way or another. I did too. No—please, Cassie, let me finish. I am no different to Julian and his mother."

"In what way?" She said slowly.

"I am also a Walker."

Cassie took a step back. "A dog?"

"No. A seal, actually. I was hoping to swim through to find you. But the Gate we went through together was closed. And I didn't even know whether it led to wherever it was Selene had taken you. I was trying to find another way. I'm so sorry, Cassie. And I'm so sorry I didn't tell you earlier that I was a Walker."

"I saw you! That day at the waterhole. You'd been swimming. I didn't realise until now, but that's what I saw!"

Ali nodded. "I wasn't sure. I thought perhaps you had. You didn't say anything. But of course, why would you have?"

"*Your kind doesn't tend to like my kind.* That's what he said to me. Julian. That was what he meant. That Walkers and Weavers don't get along."

Ali tilted her head and held Cassie in her gaze. "I knew a man once, Jack—I may have mentioned him to you before—who was both Weaver and Walker, though I didn't know it at the time. His parents must have been one of each. I don't see why it should matter what you are, what he is."

"Then why has he not spoken to me since we returned? Why won't he even look at me?"

Ali caught Cassie's hands up into her own. "Give him

time. His mother's just returned to him. And there's his father to think of, and school...so much to work out. Perhaps it's these things that keep him from you."

Cassie gazed at the grass beneath their feet, watching the fog lifting in wispy shreds under the warming sun. Perhaps.

She sighed and drew Ali into a hug. "Well, I'm glad you told me, anyway. What's another Walker in the family, after all?"

THE LAST DAYS of autumn went by in a blur. Ben began to light fires in the grates at nights and Selene had so improved that Maree decided it was time they headed back to the city. They left one chilly afternoon, promising future visits and a room at the hotel whenever Cassie or her parents had need of it.

"There'll be no more estrangement between us, Lyra. We're all we have of family now."

Cassie, who had braided Selene's hair with flowers during their last day together, received a last ferocious hug from her cousin.

"Goodbye, Cassie. Come and visit me soon. And tell Julian that I don't hate him. He's welcome to visit us too."

Ali stayed with them for a few more days before begging her leave. Her tenure at the caravan park was up, and she also had to return to the city.

"Will you keep looking for him, for Tomas?" Cassie asked her.

"Always," said Ali.

"And will you come and visit me from time to time?"

Ali laughed, her eyes bright. "Of course! Us peculiar folk

have to stick together. In fact, I was rather hoping you might like me to tutor you again next term."

"Yes, I would!"

"And your mother says that as soon as you give her back her book, she can start teaching you lessons from it."

"Oh, right."

"And apparently there's a particular subject she'd like my help with."

"What might that be?"

"I believe it's *Keeping an Eye on Walkers 101*, or something like that."

Cassie laughed. "Well, I'd be happy to skip ahead to *How not to let Walkers get you into Trouble 102*."

Ali laid her hands on Cassie's shoulders and gave her a smile that reminded her of nothing so much as Mary Poppins leaving the children for the last time.

"You've grown up in this short time, you know. I'm proud of you."

Cassie looked away, her eyes stinging.

"And don't worry about Julian. He'll come around. He feels things strongly, that one."

Cassie tilted her head to force the water back into her eyes and held her tutor's bird-like frame in a hug.

Ali squeezed her back. "I'll see you soon. Very soon."

FOR DAYS AFTER ALI LEFT, the house felt too quiet. Dad retreated into the garden and Mum, alarmingly, took up residence in the kitchen, baking, and cooking soups and curries from scratch. As Cassie had very few memories of her mum ever cooking, this did little to instil a sense of normality in the household.

One morning, skirting around the kitchen table heaped with Lyra's leathery blueberry waffles, Cassie grabbed her jacket and headed out the back gate to the Curwood. It had been weeks now; she'd given him enough time. If Julian would not come to her, then she would go to him.

Only a few yellow leaves were left clinging to the oaks and maples, their branches black sticks against the green of the eucalypts and wattles. The river was full and rushing, sweeping under the bridge in great swirls and eddies as though it had a better place to be.

The ground underfoot was sodden and vibrant with moss as she passed into the Walcotts' garden, wending her way between the old rhododendrons and up onto the white stone pathway. How long ago it seemed to her now, those days when she and Julian had played hide-and-seek amongst the roses and Violeta had enticed them to less thorny ground with her sweet treats and stories.

Cassie was at the front door before she knew it. And there, she almost lost her nerve. Her pulse was loud in her ears and her cheeks felt warm. What if he wasn't here? What if he was and he didn't want to see her? What would she say to Mr Walcott? She touched the starflower at her chest. It was warm and gave her strength. She raised the knocker and let it fall. Once, twice, a third time.

John Walcott opened the door. His face had more lines than she remembered.

"Come in," he said, stepping back to allow her inside before she'd said a word.

A moment later, she was following him down the dark hallway, their shoes scuffing softly against the flagstone floor.

"He's out in the sun-room."

Mr Walcott guided her into the lounge room and pointed

at his son. Glass doors opened out onto a roofed patio with white columns and old wisteria vines twisting up them out of cracked Grecian pots. Julian sat with his back to her on one of the wicker chairs.

"See if you can get more sense out of him than I have," he said, turning on his heel and leaving her with the· sun streaming into her eyes.

She slipped quietly out and seated herself in a chair next to Julian's. He made no move to acknowledge her presence. She followed his gaze to the forested hill beyond the Walcotts' rolling lawn.

"Is she out there?"

He lowered his eyes a fraction but did not speak.

"Do you really detest me so much, Julian?"

He turned to her, his eyes glazed and far away. Two lines appeared between his brows. "I? Detest you?"

"You have avoided me, said nothing to me since we...since—"

"Since you discovered that I'm a monster and a liar," he finished, suddenly animated, his voice dripping with derision, although whether it was for her or for himself, she couldn't tell.

"Julian, what do you take me for? Do you think I imagine Selene a beast? Or your mother?"

He let out a snort of contempt, or perhaps it was frustration. His face was clearly anguished, but she couldn't read its cause.

"Neither of them have been your lifelong friend and companion. Neither of them could possibly have loved you as I claimed to have loved you."

Cassie's faced burned. "Claimed to have? Do you not then?"

Julian pushed himself up off his chair with a short growl that sounded very dog-like.

"I have always loved you. Ever since I was a boy. It was always you. Don't you see? I ran faster for you, climbed higher for you, learned to be stronger, braver, only so that I could be worthy of you."

Cassie sat in stunned silence.

He sat down again heavily and hung his head in his hands.

She turned towards him so their knees were almost touching. "Then, I don't understand."

He looked up and drew his hair roughly back from his face with his hands. "I know you can't forgive me for lying to you the way I did. I understand that a Walker could never dream to desire you. I just...I stayed away from you because I wished it to be otherwise. Because I cannot change it, no matter how hard I wish it to be different. I thought myself a coward not telling you all these years. But now I see I was only allowing myself hope. And I couldn't see you or talk to you again after you found out because I didn't want that hope taken away."

Cassie leaned over and placed her hands on his knees, drawing herself closer to him. "Julian, that is the craziest speech I've ever heard you give. Look at me." He drew away, but she caught his hands. "No, look at me. You are not a monster or a liar, or any other horrible thing you might have heard your father call your mother, or that you might have thought yourself to be. I love you, the whole of you, just as I hope you love the whole of me. It doesn't matter what we might seem to be to the world, only what we are to each other. And you are my best friend and the boy I love."

He looked up from her hands to meet her gaze, and the

spark of hope she saw in his eyes made her heart swell into a fierce, glowing thing.

"Come here," she said, and pulled him towards her.

They fell together onto their knees on the warm patio floor. Julian brought his hands to her temples. His thumbs stroked her hair, shaking as he held her. She leaned towards the curves and angles of a face so familiar, yet in this moment so close and new.

"Cassie," he whispered, and their foreheads touched.

She closed her eyes, and when his lips met hers, she felt the wildness within him. It was sweet and strong, and it was calling her home.

Even Mr Walcott smiled as Cassie and Julian left the house together, headed to the Curwood and then, unbeknownst to his father, on to Violeta's cabin in the hills.

"I see you got through to him after all," he said. "Just be sure to have him home before sunset. There are dangerous creatures in the forest after dark."

IT RELIEVED Cassie to see Ben get back to his wood carving. He'd apparently decided that his unformed lump in the garden was not to be an animal after all.

"I think we've all had enough of beasts for a bit," he said, madly sawing off any semblance of a head.

Three days later, he led Cassie and Lyra outside with a cheerful whistle.

"Ta dah!"

In place of the ominous lump sat a lovely wooden seat, with just enough room for two, carved up and down the legs and back with curls and vines and leaves.

"For my two magical ladies," he said with a flourish and a

bow. "Now you can at least sit outside with me while I toil away in your majesties' herb garden."

Cassie allowed herself to lean against Lyra while Ben busied himself with the wheelbarrow and a pile of mulch, to breathe in her smell of smoke and tea-tree soap and home.

"Has he talked about it yet?"

Lyra pulled her in, and Cassie closed her eyes at the comforting weight of her mother's arm across her shoulders.

"No. Not yet. You know your dad. He whispers his secrets to the carrots and the runner beans. He'll be okay."

Cassie turned so she could see her mother's face. "And you? Will *you* be okay? He was your brother, after all."

Lyra gazed out across the garden. "He ceased being my brother a long time ago."

"He said I was a Darkweaver." Cassie didn't mean to say it, but the words rushed out unbidden.

Lyra shifted in the seat so that she was looking squarely at her daughter. "And what do you think?"

"I'm not sure what to think," she said, rubbing her fingers across a smooth patch in the wood.

"We all get to choose, you know," said Lyra after a minute. "Every one of us. Every day. We can choose to draw our energy from hurt and fear. Or we can choose to be in reciprocity, to receive energy with gratitude from the natural sources the world provides us. To give back in our turn. Each time we Weave, we make that choice anew. It is the sum of these choices that defines you. And no one else can make these choices for you. So no one else can define who you are. Only you."

"But Dominic said I used Darkweaving when we first met. I made the wrong choice that time."

"You did what you could to survive. You didn't know what you were doing, and I am to blame for that. If I had taught you earlier, you would have known that you had a choice to make. While I make no excuse for it, I suppose I didn't see how quickly my little girl was growing up in front of me. How ready you really were. Your dad and I, we've not done this before. We're always learning how to be parents, and there are times, like this one, when we get it plain wrong."

Cassie's fingers went to the starflower. There was a thrumming within it as though it were alive. Lyra smiled and placed her hand over Cassie's. The pendant glowed, and the vibration became almost audible, like a cat's purr.

"It seems pleased to be with you."

"I hope Maree's not too upset that Selene gave it to me."

Her mum's smile widened. "I didn't even know she had it. Our mother used to wear it all the time, as you do now. It makes me feel closer to her, knowing that it has chosen you to be its keeper. I'm sure my sister feels the same."

Ben appeared with cups of tea and a chair for himself. The long light of the afternoon caught them all in its glow, and their talk turned to other things.

As she watched the faces of her parents, Cassie knew that the tea and laughter and fragile warmth of this last autumn day would be a memory she would take with her forever. When all was dark and gone, there would still be this: Lyra and Ben and Cassie. And the fact that things had changed, that the world had shifted and could not be remade, that it was no longer the spring of Cassie's life nor the summer of theirs, only made it all the sweeter.

ACKNOWLEDGMENTS

Thank you to my beautiful friends and family. I truly couldn't do this without you.

Thank you dear Leticia and Paula for reading my early drafts, Liora and Joel for your encouragement on the business and tech front, Helen for your wonderful editing, Sue for your forensic proofing, and to Shkike (99designs) for the lovely cover.

Big love and thanks to Dan and my wonderful kiddos, Griffin and Kate. And also, of course, to Cinnamon the cat.

ALSO BY ALEXANDRA MANFIELD

The River Daughter (2020)

Orion's Web (2022)

If you'd like to find out more, please visit:

www.spindlepress.com.au